DRY HEAT

DRY HEAT

•

Meagan J. Meehan

AVALON BOOKS
NEW YORK

Published by Thomas Bouregy & Co., Inc.
160 Madison Avenue, New York, NY 10016

Library of Congress Cataloging-in-Publication Data

Meehan, Meagan J.
   Dry heat / Meagan J. Meehan.
        p. cm.
   ISBN 978-0-8034-7751-3 (acid-free.paper)
   I. Title.
   PS3613.E368D79 2009
   813'.6—dc22
                                    2009024254

PRINTED IN THE UNITED STATES OF AMERICA
ON ACID-FREE PAPER
BY HADDON CRAFTSMEN, BLOOMSBURG, PENNSYLVANIA

This book is dedicated to my wonderful parents,
Michael and Mary.
And to my Uncle Stan, the Wild West fan.

Chapter One

"It's hotter than a coal fire out here, I feel like an egg in a fryin' pan!" Willis Lauder declared, half whining and half shouting. Sheriff Phil Palmer didn't know about the rest of his posse but he was having trouble keeping his cool while dealing with the squirrelly banker turned hunter-for-a-day.

"Yeah, Will," the sheriff began, smiling as he shortened the banker's name; Willis hated it when people shortened his name. "We know it's hot, we're all out here with you."

The sheriff's sarcasm made the other men smirk and Willis' scowl deepen. Willis Lauder was a short and stocky man of middle age. His balding blond hair was obscured under his ten-gallon hat and his wrinkled face was weathered from constant complaining and frowning. His view on life was as gray as his eyes and, if it

1

hadn't been for his general honesty as a banker, he would probably be one of the most disliked people in town.

Although, it *was* hot in the midday sun; Willis had a point there. Mirage water glistened upon the desert sand and the cloudless blue sky stretched endlessly above the dry plains. The sun beat mercilessly upon the six-man posse crouching in a tangle of dry shrubs. It was the kind of dry heat which made the New Mexico air hard to breathe. There was no dampness, no precipitation; nothing but hot dry air, cactuses, and cattle bones. Off in the distance stood the Sand Sun Mountains, looming masses of reddish-brown earth dotted with caves, loose rocks, small shrubs, and cougars.

"But I'm tellin' y'all I'm roastin' like a chicken on a spit! How much longer do we gotta stay out here?" Willis demanded, his nasal voice echoing between the canyons. Fifty yards behind him the posse's horses neighed and fidgeted, unhappy to be tied to a tall cactus and forced to stay put in such heat.

"It takes as long as it takes, Will," Phil snapped, once again making sure to elongate the word *Will*. "You want somebody else to get killed on account of that cougar who went bad for blood?"

Silence from Willis, a momentary victory.

Phil sighed as he wiped the sweat off of his brow; this was no way to spend a Monday or start off the week. The sheriff was a tall, middle-aged, middle-weight man whose face had wrinkled prematurely. His graying brown hair, which hung to his shoulders, needed to be both washed and cut. His hazel eyes were red from sand, heat, and staring up at the same canyon for too long in the bright midday sun. His nerves were slowly but surely giving out on him—this time on account of a cougar.

Cougars. Phil Palmer reckoned that if he never saw or heard about another cougar again it would be too soon. A cougar was the reason he was stuck out in the desert in his thick leather boots, ten-gallon hat and heavy gunbelt, sweating like an animal and fighting heatstroke. In the past week half a dozen cattle and one young ranch-hand—a nineteen-year-old drifter named Rob—had been mauled to death; cougar teeth marks were clearly embedded on each of the carcasses. Old-timers who had seen such deaths before thought the animal had a lust for blood and, unless it was caught and killed, its need to kill would grow only stronger. Phil was well aware that a blood-crazed cougar was something which could easily instigate a panic and, in a small town like Dry Heat, panic was just about the most dangerous thing that could happen.

Dry Heat's a good name for the town, Phil thought as he squirmed with discomfort. He was a lawman. He was supposed to be a figure of control and perseverance but, darn it, he was hot! He had been crouched behind a large shrub for what seemed like an eternity. He wanted this hunt to be over. He wanted to shoot the cougar dead and go back to his office where he could lie back in his chair, barefoot, in his undershirt and jeans. To the devil with the image of a constantly controlled sheriff; Phil was a real flesh and blood man and real men got hot in one-hundred-and-five-degree weather. Plus, at forty-seven years of age, crouching and bending wasn't exactly good for his back.

"Well I didn't mean to make y'all sore, I was just sayin' that it's hot out here an' we ain't seen nothin' all mornin'." There it was again, the high, nagging voice of Willis.

"Yes, Will, I've also noticed we've been sittin' here since dawn an' ain't seen nothin' yet; thanks for remindin' me."

Deputy Ron Harris shot a quick glance over at the sheriff. Ron was a twenty-four-year-old, medium-sized redhead. It was obvious that the deputy was biting the insides of his cheeks to suppress a laugh as he listened to the dialogue between Willis and the sheriff. All morning Phil had been taking potshots at Willis and the wordy standoff was striking Ron as funnier and funnier with every hour that passed. It seemed as if the more annoyed both Phil and Willis got, the harder Ron had to try not to burst out laughing.

Yet, Phil really was getting angry at the banker's comments. A young man had died a horrible death on account of the animal they were hunting and all Willis could think about was his own discomfort. The sheriff was tired and hot too—all the men were—but no one else was openly voicing their frustration.

"Just as long as y'all know how bad this heat is, a man could die from this!" Willis declared, unable to keep from complaining, as he guzzled water from his canteen.

I'm never taking another banker on a hunt as long as I live. If that cougar was anywhere near here he's scared the darn thing away by now, Phil thought and bit his tongue to keep himself from launching into a tirade against Willis.

Still, the sheriff reckoned that it wouldn't be right to snap at any of these men who had volunteered to help capture the cougar. Phil Palmer and Ron Harris were the only two lawmen in Dry Heat and, technically, the only two people required to deal with emergency situations. However, around Dry Heat people looked out for one another. When the sheriff and the deputy had requested aid they had received it—Willis Lauder, Nick Stooker, Michael Bonvey, and Dwayne Roberts had all stepped forward to help the town lawmen.

Nick Stooker was the town shoemaker. A tall, burly, yet good-hearted man in his mid-twenties, Nick was easy to like.

Michael Bonvey was the town blacksmith. He was a portly, muscular, round-faced man in his early forties who was fast with a joke and generally likable, despite the fact that he could be hot-headed.

At twenty-two, Dwayne Roberts was the youngest man in the group. He was a slightly built ranch hand with thick black hair and piercing blue eyes who was quick with a smile and even quicker to help someone in need. Yet, he was also known to be slightly simpleminded and trusting; in other words, easy to fool. Dwayne was usually the object of both jokes and pity amongst the townsfolk for two reasons: His lacking intelligence and the woman he had married—one of the infamous Hubbards.

Dwayne wasn't the only ranch hand who had volunteered to come on this hunt. Despite the offers, both the sheriff and the deputy reckoned that the majority of ranch hands were better off looking after their livestock. All evidence showed that this cougar had been after cattle and the unfortunate Rob had been killed as a second thought; probably because he had posed a threat to the animal. Of course, any rancher with a shred of sense was always armed and alert. Rob had been armed but his gun had jammed, so he had no way to defend himself when the attack occurred.

Phil stared at the raw jackrabbit meat lying in the center of the desert about thirty yards in front of his posse. He had shot and skinned those rabbits to use as cougar bait and so far nothing but a few buzzards had come by. If the meat stayed out in the heat much longer it would surely spoil.

So much for Mr. Bunny givin' his life for a good cause, Phil thought as he removed his canteen from his belt and swallowed the last drop of water. Looking down at his empty canteen, cynical thoughts arose in his mind. *If we stay out here much longer maybe I'll die an' then they can strip me and lay me down there an' use me as bait. We already know this thing don't mind eatin' people meat.*

"Hey, Sheriff, is your niece still comin' to town?" Dwayne asked suddenly, breaking the desert-day silence.

"Yup."

"This Saturday, right?"

"Yup."

"Shame about her folks."

"How do you know all this?" Phil snapped, not wanting to think about Cynthia.

"People talk."

"Well, we ain't talkin' here, keep your voice down or that cougar ain't never gonna be seen."

"Just makin' conversation. We ain't seen nothin' yet an' probably won't," Dwayne whined.

"Don't you start!" the sheriff snapped. He could only take so much complaining in one day.

It was true that his brother Clyde's daughter, Cynthia, was arriving in Dry Heat on Saturday via the mail train. Phil had never met her but he knew that she was thirteen years old and newly orphaned. Both her folks and her little brother had died of consumption back in New Jersey; Cynthia had remained uninfected by pure miracle. Phil had no idea how he was supposed to raise a little girl like her and the question had caused him more than a few sleepless nights.

It's a mistake taking her here, a bad mistake, especially now that Tulmacher's runnin' around causin' a commotion.

Larry Tulmacher was a heavyset man, newly arrived from the south, looking to make himself mayor of Dry Heat. He and his sleazy, scruffy cohorts gave Phil the creeps, but Tulmacher always seemed so in control and pleasant that it was hard to simply run him out of town.

Plus, the man could talk fancy and the townspeople fell for his speeches the way rain fell from clouds. Heck, the townspeople loved him so much that he had been awarded the key to the town a few days before. The sheriff sighed; recently it seemed as if too much was going on in Dry Heat—none of it good.

The sunlight was getting deeper, cooler in temperature yet warmer in color as midday turned into late afternoon. Phil decided to give the lingering hunt only another few hours, there was no use staying out until dark. Craning his head around, Phil looked back at the horses. Crow, the sheriff's trusty black stallion, was standing in place, swaying his long tail from side to side. Next to Crow was Nita, Deputy Ron's buckskin mare. She was waving her head slightly in the breeze, bored. Willi's, Nick's, Michael's, and Dwayne's horses stood idly by as well; all six of the animals looked hot and unhappy. *That makes an even dozen of us,* Phil thought before turning his attention back to the plains.

"How do you know that critter is even gonna come by this way?" Nick asked as he stood and stretched his back.

"It was spotted 'round here," Ron replied. "We figure the meat will attract it."

"Wasn't he also seen up near the mountains?" Michael asked.

"Seen by who?" Phil questioned, suddenly intrigued.

"My son-in-law's a rancher an' he said that he seen that cougar actin' all funny up on the Sand Sun."

"Your son-in-law ain't no rancher, he's a chicken farmer!" Willis sneered.

"Exactly, that cougar came after his chickens in broad daylight an' he chased the dang thing away with a shotgun an' it ran up to them mountains!"

"Why didn't he shoot it?" Nick demanded to know.

"He shot at it but God knows Dean can't aim worth a penny, so it was the noise that scared it away more than anythin' else."

"I don't give a flyin' saddle horn about his aim! Just tell me why you never mentioned this before!" Phil declared, more than a little annoyed.

"No one asked me. I knew we was comin' in this general direction and that's where it'd been seen. I thought y'all knew more about it than I did. An' no one believed Dean when he said he'd seen it."

"That's 'cause Dean drinks too dang much," Willis proclaimed.

"Well if you had told somebody then we could have started up on them mountains by now, checking through caves instead of just watchin' over this here plain all day!" the sheriff declared. He felt robbed of a day's worth of work and a year's worth of energy.

"Ain't that dangerous?" Dwayne questioned.

"Course its dangerous!" Phil shouted. "But so's that animal!"

"Well, if you're such a good tracker, why didn't you think of them caves?"

"I never claimed to be no good tracker! Besides, cougars, especially crazed ones who ain't thinkin' half right, can live other places besides caves. This here clearin' was the only place I thought it had been seen!"

"Well, I'm sick and tired of waitin' out here for some-thin' that ain't gonna come!" Willis shouted. Phil sighed; he had temporarily forgotten the banker's presence. "I ain't complainin' half as much as I should be!"

"Dang fool," Phil muttered.

"What?" Willis shrieked.

"Dang cruel heat," the sheriff replied. "It's an old ex-pression of my mother's."

"No, you didn't say that, you called me a dang fool!"

"I did not."

"Yes, you did!"

"You callin' me a liar?"

"I guess I am since you're lyin'!"

Deputy Ron realized that, after five hours in the sun, tempers were starting to flare. He was planning to break up the fight when he saw a sudden movement out of the corner of his eye. Something was moving fast up on the Sand Sun Mountains. Automatically, Ron stiffened his posture, alert. None of the other men noticed.

"I see somethin' y'all," Ron announced but his words fell unnoticed among the bickering men.

"You've always had a mean attitude!" Willis was shouting at Phil.

"An' you have always been a no-good whiner!" the sheriff shouted back.

"Well, I think you both got each other pegged," Nick declared.

"You ain't no sweet sugar neither," Michael snapped at Nick.

"Y'all . . ." Ron said a bit louder, his voice trailing off unheard.

"Well, I can't stand none of you! Y'all a bunch of lunatics!" Phil spit angrily.

"Y'all!" Ron shouted.

"What?" Phil screamed, turning to the deputy.

"There's movement on the mountaintop."

"What?"

"Up there," Ron replied pointing toward the Sand Sun Mountains, "somethin's runnin' 'round in circles, all messed up lookin'." Silence fell over the group as the men turned to peer up at the mountains.

"Ain't runnin' in circles a sure sign of an animal gone bad?" Nick asked.

"Sure is," Michael replied.

The men glared up at the mountaintop intensely. The only sound was their breathing; the only movement was their bellies rising and falling to the rhythm of their breath. One minute passed, then two, three, four, five, six—the cougar dashed across the mountaintop. Its movements were harsh and jerky; the animal moved without direction in a tormented trot.

She's a sick one allright. Phil felt a pang of pity for the animal. He was not a man who enjoyed killing, but looking at the state the cougar was in, it became clear that shooting it was not only absolutely necessary, it was also merciful.

"Can you get clear aim from here?" the deputy asked the sheriff. "You're a better shot than me."

"Don't reckon so but I'm gonna try," Phil replied as he positioned his rifle. The cougar was moving in a circular motion, shaking its foamy-mouthed head from side to side as it ran.

It was hard to get a clear shot at the animal since it was moving fast and unpredictable. Phil wanted to shoot this cougar dead; he didn't want to wound it. The creature had suffered enough already. Taking a deep breath, Phil aimed and pulled the trigger—and hit rock. The impact sprayed gravel in every direction. Phil had missed the cougar by a good three feet. The cougar turned around and, still shaking and jerking, fled into an opening in the mountain. The sheriff jumped up immediately, slung his gun over his shoulder and hastily moved toward the mountains.

"Where the heck are you goin'?" Willis demanded to know.

"I missed, it went into the cave, I gotta follow it," the sheriff replied.

"Why can't we just wait for it to come out again?" Nick asked.

"Because that might be hours away from now, provided it don't have another way to get out," Phil snapped, feeling as if he was losing valuable time talking. "Come on, all of you, let's go."

"Now wait just a second!" Nick shouted. "I didn't know nothin' about gettin' so close to it. This seems mighty dangerous to me, an' I won't lie, I can't afford to go getting myself killed; not with Rose eight months gone with child for the first time an' all." Nick's tone of voice was apologetic but it was clear from his gaze that his decision had been made.

"Don't worry about it, Nick," Ron replied. "You stay here with the horses. They need lookin' after anyway; we don't want no thieves runnin' off with 'em."

"I'll whistle a signal to you when you're needed," the sheriff added.

"Thank you," Nick replied sincerely before he turned toward the horses.

"The rest of you comin'?" Phil asked. Ron was already beside him, and Michael and Dwayne were walking toward the mountains without question. Willis lingered, unsure.

"Well, Will, comin'?"

"Heck, might as well," Willis replied, gathering up his gun and kicking the sand with his feet. "This ain't no way to die, but I don't want nobody thinkin' I'm a coward."

"You'll get a brave man's grave," Ron replied, trying hard to hide his sarcasm.

I don't know about a brave one but he'll need a grave allright if he don't quit his whinin' mighty soon, Phil thought, as he and his small posse walked toward the Sand Sun Mountains.

The terrain was rough and rugged; gravel crunched under leather boots with each step. The reddish-orange afternoon sun reflected off the mountain, giving the men the impression that they were walking on fire. Climbing upwards was difficult since the sand was laced with small rocks and there were few places to secure a foothold. Phil staggered up the mountain, grabbing at brush and frantically lunging forward. He was afraid of losing his balance, falling backwards, and breaking either his neck or his back. The sheriff's hands were cut and bruised in a number of places before he was able to reach a secure flat spot feet away from the cave's entrance. Taking a few resting breaths, Phil examined his hands and wondered from how far away cougars could smell blood, especially crazed ones. Would the smell of blood make it more prone to attack? He had been born and raised out West but he knew little about cougars, let alone ones with a blood lust. He had never been forced to deal with an issue like this before, and he found the unfamiliar situation more than a little intimidating.

The other men were still struggling to reach the sheriff; balancing themselves and their weapons was not an easy task. Several times Phil saw some gravel give way and one of his posse members lose some footing. Even Willis had stopped his yakking in order to concentrate on not falling.

"Dang, what a trek!" Ron declared when he finally reached Phil, followed closely by the other men. Although the younger men took time to catch their breath, Phil couldn't help but think how winded he was now compared to what he would have been only a few years ago. *Old age is comin' on fast.* As if to discredit the thought, he stood up.

"Come on you bunch of slackers, I'm older than y'all an' I'm ready to go faster!" the sheriff stated, staring at the narrow path of rock his posse would have to walk in order to get to the cave.

"But you've had more restin' time!" Willis protested, as he guzzled water from his canteen.

"Will," Phil began, finally reaching his limit, "if you don't stop your belly achin' I will personally see to it that you are this cougar's last meal."

"Don't you threaten me—"

"Come on y'all," Ron spoke up, giving Willis a hefty tap on the back, thus stopping a new argument from beginning, "we got us a crazed critter to deal with."

"It's a big, vicious animal! It ain't no critter!" Willis snapped, needing to have the last word.

Ignoring Willis, the men walked in a row, carefully navigating around the mountain. Phil was leading the pack. He was trying to remain calm but he was nervous, very nervous. The cougar could jump out at him at any moment, and his reflexes weren't as good as they had once been. Out of habit the sheriff ran his hands over his stubbly face; shaving was not something he was fond of doing nor was it a commonplace activity for men around Dry Heat. Behind him, Ron watched the sheriff rub his face; the action made him uneasy. The deputy knew the sheriff better than anyone, and he knew that Phil didn't rub his hands over his face like that unless something had really gotten under his skin. *He's scared*, Ron thought and shivered. The sheriff was the bravest man he had ever known, and if he was scared, then God help the rest of them.

Sidestepping around a particularly narrow ledge of rock, Phil saw the cave's opening. It was a black hole in the red rock, wide and open like a hungry mouth. Phil slowed and signaled for his men to do the same. Near the cave's entrance the width of the ledge was wider, allowing the men more space to walk on.

"Okay, y'all draw your weapons, we gonna be needin' them in a second or two."

From behind him Phil heard guns being unslung and cocked. The sheriff grabbed his own gun, positioned it in front of him, and held it tightly. He never took his eyes off the cave's entrance. It was too dark to see inside and anything could be lurking in the doorway shadows, waiting to pounce. Phil grappled with the small lantern he had brought with him. While fumbling in his pockets for his matches, the sheriff spoke to his posse.

"I have to light this thing, say my prayers, an' go in for the kill. If that cougar is in there, I best kill it now before it can rip all our throats out for dinner an' then go have Nick an' the horses for dessert. This here is a dangerous thing to do; I'm gonna need lots of cover from you boys back there. If you hear me yellin' start shootin', you hear? I'd rather die by a bullet than be eaten alive by a cougar."

Phil stole a quick glance over his shoulder to ensure that his men were ready with their weapons. Satisfied with the backup his men were supplying, Phil struck a match, lit the lantern, and—with a quick prayer of *Please Lord let me do right here*—descended into the cave.

It all happened so fast that the sheriff had no time to

be afraid. One second he was in the cave, gripping his gun and swinging his lantern around, and the next moment he was listening to a low, steady growl. Phil quickly swung his lantern to the left and saw the glowing eyes of the cougar. Its ears were down, its foaming mouth was twisted into a snarl, and it was crouched, ready for attack. Without thinking, Phil gripped his rifle and pulled the trigger. The combination of dark and lack of concentration diverted his aim. The bullet flew into the high wall and ceiling, spraying pebbles everywhere. The sudden noise startled the cougar which, uninjured, ran for the cave's exit, disregarding Sheriff Phil.

"Look out, she's comin' towards y'all!" Phil roared to his men. From where he stood he could see the cougar's descent toward the light of the outdoors. He could hear it snarling as it ran from the cold darkness of the cave into the warm light of the afternoon sun. He watched as it observed the four men before it, hunched down, and pounced. Then he was running toward the outside of the cave, praying no one would be killed.

Before Phil could get to the front of the cave, the cougar had leaped at Michael. The animal was moving so fast that Michael was unable to aim well and fired his bullet into the stone atop the cave's entrance. With debris raining down upon him, Michael lifted his gun and swung it like a club. The butt of the gun connected to the side of the cougar's head, causing the snarling creature to yelp and fall. Yet this animal was strong, angry, and crazy, and almost as soon as it fell it got back up and ran toward Michael. Taking one end of the gun in each hand, Michael held his rifle in front of him and used it as a barrier between himself and the snarling cougar; a cross-held gun was all that separated life from death.

The entire scene had taken only about ten seconds, but it seemed much longer. As the sheriff grappled with his gun and ran towards the front of the cave, he saw the position of each member of his posse clearly. Michael was wrestling with the snarling cougar. He was screaming and pleading for someone to shoot it. Ron was holding his rifle, tightly aiming for a safe shot so he didn't shoot Michael. Dwayne was grappling with his gun, but he was scared and shaking and kept dropping the weapon on the ground. Willis was standing to the side, his gun held out in front of him, but he was shaking too badly to aim or shoot; instead he was screaming in a high womanly voice for God almighty to come save him.

POW!

The sound of the gunshot echoed down the cave's corridor. Instantly the cougar fell to the ground, dead. It had been shot straight through the skull. The deputy stood over his fresh kill triumphantly as Michael sat on the ground, his eyes wide with a mixture of terror and relief. Dwayne stared at the dead cougar as if it was some kind of freak. Willis screamed thankful praise to God for saving them.

"Good shot, pardner," Phil declared and gave Ron a congratulory slap on the back. "I'll signal Nick to bring the horses over this way. We'll carry this menace's carcass back to town an' show the people that this cougar ain't gonna be no more bother."

After giving the deputy another pat on the back, Sheriff Phil walked over to the mountain's edge. He could clearly see Nick in the distance, sitting under the shade of the horses. The sheriff put his hands to his mouth and let out a high-pitched whistle. The sound quickly reached Nick, who looked up, waved, and prepared to bring the horses to the foot of the mountain. As he watched Nick get the horses ready to move, Phil smiled. It had been a long, hard, and tiring day, but it had all been worth it in the end.

It all went well after all, the sheriff thought happily as he turned around and walked back toward the other men.

Twenty minutes later, Nick and the horses waited at the bottom of the mountain as the five men atop it debated how to get the cougar's body down with them. The dead animal was much heavier than they had expected.

"I ain't touchin' that thing!" Willis shrieked, pointing at what was left of the cougar.

"You don't have to, Will." Phil was considerably calmer and in much better spirits now that the stress of finding the cougar was gone. "You're queasy and I have a bad back so we'll carry the guns down, Ron an' Michael will carry the cougar since they're the strong ones here, an' Dwayne will carry the lantern. Sound good?"

"Fine!" Willis snapped, obviously unhappy with being spoken to like a child. "An' I ain't queasy! I just don't like the idea of gettin' a dead animal scent all over my clothes!"

Ignoring Willis, Ron picked up the cougar's front legs, and Michael picked up its back legs. Slowly and carefully, the two men began their descent. Phil and Willis followed carrying the guns as Dwayne tagged along behind the other men carrying the small lantern.

"An' I don't care what crazy thoughts are swirlin' 'round that head of yours," Willis informed the sheriff, "I ain't carryin' that thing on the back of my horse!"

"I wouldn't dream of makin' you do that, Will. I'll carry the carcass on the back of my horse for you, okay?" Phil was too tired to argue; at this point it was easier to patronize.

"Fine!"

At long last Willis was content enough to remain silent. Phil sighed and tried to ignore his throbbing arms, which were exhausted from carrying the heavy guns. He looked ahead to see Nick waiting patiently with the horses and Ron and Michael huffing and puffing as they carried the dead weight of the cougar. *At least we ain't goin' uphill.* Phil smiled to himself, unable to resist his good mood. He had avoided killing Willis, he'd seen a blood-crazed cougar hunted down and killed—although he did regret not getting to plant the bullet in the varmint himself—and he had saved the lives of more people and cattle by doing so. It was approaching dusk now. Once they got the carcass strapped onto the back of Crow, they could ride straight back to town and be there before nightfall.

Won't it be a fine thing to step into Claire's Cactus Saloon and have a cold drink an' finally get these danged

*boots and gunbelt off. Yup, it's gonna be mighty nice to be
in that saloon, cooling off an' playing some cards an'—*

A thud followed by a piercing scream rose from behind, jostling the sheriff out of his thoughts. He turned
around to see Dwayne lying on the ground, screaming in
agony and holding his throat. A hissing snake was slith-
ering away, its tail rattling. With sudden horror, Phil realized that Dwayne had lost his footing, tripped, and
fallen beside a rattlesnake. Surprised and scared, the
venomous creature retaliated by biting him on the neck.
Blood was pouring out from between Dwayne's fingers
on the hand which held his wounded neck. He was
screaming but the scream was fast becoming a gurgle.
Dwayne's eyes were rolling wildly in his skull. He was
trying to move but was only able to make twisting, jerky
motions.

The other men had seen what happened. Ron and
Michael dropped the carcass and ran toward Dwayne.
Nick left the horses standing and ran as fast as he could
up the mountain towards the injured man. Willis was
taking tentative steps toward the scene, darting his
eyes around frantically, making absolutely sure that the
rattlesnake was gone. Phil was the first one by Dwayne's
side. He was trying to tie his pocket handkerchief around
Dwayne's neck to keep the bloody wound from spurt-
ing. Dwayne was groaning and twitching his feet. His
eyes were large and scared, pleading for the other men
to help him.

"We need a doctor!" the deputy screamed, his usually
calm voice rising with panic.

"I could ride back to town an' get one!" Nick offered, still panting from the effort of his quick ascent.

"Katie," Dwayne whispered weakly.

"It's all right partner, you're gonna be just fine," Phil stated in the calmest voice he could muster, loathing every word of the lie but not knowing what else to do or say. With much effort Dwayne reached his hand out, grabbed the side of Phil's shirt, and squeezed. Then, his eyes tilted upwards toward the sky. Sighing, he loosened his grip on the sheriff's shirt, and took his final breath. Phil's lying words were the last ones Dwayne Roberts would ever hear.

"Really, y'all, I mean it, I could get goin' right now an' get the doctor to ride back here an' help 'em," Nick was repeating, his voice laced with panic.

"No need," Phil cut in, "no doctor will help him now."

"He's dead?" Michael asked, unable to believe it even as he stared into the dead man's face.

"I knew this trip would end in death!" Willis wailed.

"Shut your mouth, Will," Ron ordered, turning to flash the banker a hard, cold stare. Something about the expression on the young deputy's face, coupled with the tone of his voice, made Willis obey him.

The men silently stood over Dwayne's corpse for a handful of minutes which seemed like a number of hours. It was Nick who finally broke the silence: "This is gonna send Katie straight over the edge."

Chapter Two

Katelyn "Katie" Hubbard Roberts was from a bad family; that was the first and foremost fact known about her. It was common knowledge throughout Dry Heat that all the Hubbards had evil criminal minds. They robbed banks and stole horses, drank too much and got into bar fights which ended in body counts. Within the past thirty years, six Hubbard men had been hanged for violent crimes.

The Hubbards had come to Dry Heat when Phil was a small boy. They had built a shack so far on the out-skirts of the town that no one even considered them members of Dry Heat. The Hubbards, especially the Hubbard women, weren't sociable people. They hardly ever came into town and, whenever they did, it was only to shop for fabrics or other essential items delivered by train. It was obvious that the female portion of the Hubbards only came into town when they had no other option, and it was equally obvious that they passionately hated the unavoidable trips. They spent every second in Dry Heat shifting their eyes around and mumbling to one another. It was as if they believed the townspeople were fixing to lynch them just for showing their faces. Noting how skinny the women were and the tattered clothing they wore, Phil reckoned that the Hubbard family survived mainly on the meager rations they were able to gather from the desert and their ability to sew old garments. After all, buying food and new clothes would require a trip to town, and that was not a favorable option.

Unlike the Hubbard women, the Hubbard men would occasionally come into town willingly—primarily to drink at the saloon. The Hubbards were mean drunks, and it was painfully clear that they were also thieves. They took long trips and always returned with the finest horses, clothes, and weapons—hardly the luxuries of poor ranchers. As a boy, Phil had wondered why the law didn't step down on the Hubbard men. It was obvious they were thieves, and it wouldn't have been a hard fact to prove. Yet, at the time in question, Dry Heat was a fairly new town and its sheriff was a weak, cowardly man who felt that, as long as the Hubbards didn't rob his town, their suspicious wealth was none of his concern. Phil was ashamed to admit that the weak cowardly sheriff had been his own Uncle Henry, who was more interested in having a badge and the prestige that

came along with it than performing a lawman's dangerous duties.

Phil's father, Len, had been a cattle rancher and every
few months Len, teenaged Phil, and a few hired cowboys
had taken cattle forty to sixty miles east to market. Although Phil had loved those weeklong journeys, he had
hated passing the Hubbard property. It was usually an unnerving experience since it seemed that one thousand
eyes were glaring hatefully at him every time he rode by.
Phil clearly remembered seeing dirty and barefoot children in tattered clothing staring at him from around
corners or in between cracks in the shack wood. There
were more people in the Hubbard family than could be
counted, and it was hard to tell which woman had which
child by which man. The kids were usually fighting, and
the women were always pregnant; usually by rough-
housing drifters they had come across and turned into
husbands. The shack was dirty and it smelled like pig
manure—unsurprising considering that the shack was
built for a family of five and, at very least, fifteen Hubbards were holed up in there at once.

For years the Hubbards were ignored by the people
of Dry Heat. They were hardly ever spoken about or
thought about; they were simply forsaken like the black
sheep they were. The Hubbards stayed on the outskirts of
town, laying so low that they were almost invisible. No
one knew anything about them and they didn't know
anything about anyone in town, and that was the way both
sides liked it.

Then, fourteen-year-old Dwayne Roberts and his

parents came to Dry Heat and built a home on the edge of town. Dwayne was the only surviving child of Mary, a quiltmaker, and Gerald, a coal miner, who wanted to move further west to start new, happier lives after losing three children. Dwayne's two brothers had died in infancy and his sister had succumbed to scarlet fever when she was twelve. Dwayne had also suffered from scarlet fever but, after weeks of sickness, he had slowly recovered. Mary and Gerald were so grateful to God to have one child left that they often overlooked Dwayne's limited mental capacity, and this proved to be a foolish mistake.

Dwayne was a nice boy. He was strong, good-natured, and honest but he had trouble reading people. He believed that everyone wanted to be his friend and he didn't understand concepts such as manipulation and deceit. Most of all, Dwayne was lonely, and he searched endlessly for a girl to spend time with. Dwayne was painfully shy around the opposite sex, but he still made an effort to be friendly with them. Phil remembered a younger version of the now-deceased Dwayne desperately trying to get young women to dance with him at town functions. He wasn't particularly bad looking but, because of his "dumb" label and his tendency to be somewhat awkward, he was almost always turned down. On the rare occasion when a young lady agreed to dance with him it was an action done purely out of pity, and they refused to give him a second glance after the song ended. Phil had watched these scenes from a distance, and he always felt a great deal of pity for poor Dwayne, the outcast.

The rumors that fifteen-year-old Dwayne was lusting after one of the Hubbard girls came as absolutely no surprise to the sheriff. Dwayne had been in Dry Heat for over a year and lived less than a mile away from the Hubbards—a family blessed with many women, some of whom were mighty nice to look at. Phil could see why a Hubbard girl would appeal to Dwayne. They never went into town to attend dances or socialize; in fact, they tried to avoid the town at all costs. They had never laughed at him or refused him a dance—heck, they were never even at the dances to watch his failed courtship attempts!

Sixteen-year-old Katie turned out to be the object of Dwayne's interest. Katie was probably the prettiest of the Hubbard girls with her red hair, small frame, freckled skin, and fiery brown eyes. She was definitely the most manipulative. When Dwayne finally got the courage to approach her she came onto him . . . hard.

Phil had been resting in his office one day when Dwayne's extremely distraught mother burst through the door. Mary Roberts had cried and wailed to Phil that her simple son was being seduced by a trollop and declared that she wanted the sheriff's help in getting Dwayne away from Katie. Phil had listened to Mary's worries, nodded in all the right places, and patted her shoulder comfortingly, but he had been unable to offer her help.

"I'm afraid I see nothin' I can do," he had told her, trying to sound as gentle and sympathetic as possible. "No laws are bein' broken, ma'am."

"But she's trappin' him, seducin' him, an' he ain't even got the right sense in his head to see what she's doin' to him!" Mary had screamed, her voice breaking with outrage. "They go for walks out on the range for hours. Do you think I don't know what they're doin' out there all day?"

All Phil had been able to do was watch and listen until Mary finally became so flustered and frustrated that she marched out of his office and slammed the door shut behind her. Phil had felt bad about not being more of a help, but he couldn't arrest Katie for flirting with a boy. Besides, the law was already having enough trouble with Katie's cousins and brothers, who had grown from ruthless boys into lawless men.

Word had it that Katie's cousin Earl, a pudgy boy with a pimply face and a lisp, had gone out of town to steal a bunch of horses and had been shot dead by the animals' owners. Then Katie's brother, Shawn, a lanky, husky-voiced bully, had killed a man in a barroom brawl in a town about sixty miles north of Dry Heat. He was tried and hanged shortly after it was discovered that, aside from being a drunk with a quick fist, Shawn was also a card cheat; he had been scamming cowboys in rigged poker games for weeks. Yes, sir, the Hubbard boys were hard enough to deal with without adding a Hubbard girl into the mix.

Six months after Mary Roberts had come crying to

Sheriff Phil her worst nightmare came true—sixteen-year-old Dwayne announced that he and Katie were going to get married and that he had already started building them a small house out on the range. He said it would be an extra special day because Katie had agreed to get married in the Dry Heat town church. On both sides the news had caused bitter feelings and tempers to flare. The Roberts' blamed Katie, claiming that she had pushed their son into the marriage. The Hubbards said that Dwayne was a no-good excuse for a man who didn't have one ounce of gall. Gall, in the Hubbard family circle, meant not giving two hoots about breaking laws and causing mayhem. For a good six weeks the wedding of Dwayne and Katie was the prime source of gossip in Dry Heat. The Hubbards said the Roberts were stuck-up liars; the Roberts said the Hubbards were trash and the townspeople sided with the Roberts'.

The wedding was an outright disaster. Katie and Dwayne were married by Preacher Warren Harden in the little white church in Dry Heat. The ceremony was less than magical. When the time came for anyone against the marriage to speak, Preacher Warren had been forced to listen to the ranting objections of practically everyone in the church. Katie, who always had a dangerously angry edge to her personality, had screamed at all of her guests that she and Dwayne would be married whether they liked the idea or not. Dwayne had simply stood at the altar, looking around unhappily, wondering how anyone could disapprove of the love he felt for Katie. Finally, due to a lack of a probable reason in the eyes of God not to marry the couple, Preacher Warren had pronounced Dwayne and Katie husband and wife as family members wailed and sobbed, cussed and bickered. The reception had been worse. What was supposed to have been a joyful outdoor celebration in the church courtyard turned into a scene resembling a Civil War battle. Chairs were thrown, tables were turned over, and fists flew. The cowboys serving as the reception's musical entertainment ran, protectively clutching their guitars, for their safety as the Hubbards, the Roberts, and the townspeople battled it out. The fight became so unruly and outrageous that Sheriff Phil had been forced to end the reception half an hour after it had begun.

Dwayne's wedding had driven a deep wedge between him and his parents. He refused to speak to them for two years after he married Katie. When they passed one another in town, not a single "howdy" was uttered. Mary and Gerald Roberts cussed God for taking all of their children from them—three in death and one in marriage—and they eventually moved away from Dry Heat, no one knew where to. Phil reckoned that they would never know about Dwayne's death.

The Hubbards, enraged by the marriage of their daughter to a "townie," had packed up and left Dry Heat two days after the wedding. The townspeople were ecstatic. Overnight, the 30-year Hubbard problem had ended; they were finally gone—all but Katie. She and Dwayne moved into their newly built home on the edge of town. As the last Hubbard in Dry Heat, Katie quickly grew paranoid, believing that if she ever showed her face in town again she would be killed due to the memories people kept regarding her roots. Thus, Dwayne was the one who had to do all of the town errands.

Most people said that Katie had married Dwayne only because he was a hard worker and she knew he would make money. The same people said that Dwayne had gone along with the marriage because he was too soft-headed to have known any better. Yet anyone who heard Dwayne talk about his wife wondered how accurate those beliefs were. Katie obviously treated Dwayne right; she cooked for him and mended his clothes. Dwayne was madly in love with Katie, that fact was clear from miles away. He provided well for her, he made sure she always had shoes, good clothes, and fresh food to cook with. He was obsessed with making absolutely sure the house was well maintained, and he paid attention to her—good, loving, respectful attention—not the raw, butt-pinching and hollering attention her uncles, cousins, brothers, and father had plied her with. Dwayne was fixated on keeping Katie happy. He never held her family's past against her, and he made sure that her life was worlds better than it had been growing up. Dwayne wasn't a smart man or a sly man but he was a good man, and he was an escape for Katie. Having him meant that she could avoid her family while still staying away from mingling with the townsfolk. It was the good living he offered her and the sweet way he looked and spoke to her that made Katie love Dwayne. It was also what made her wail like a dying dog when she saw Dwayne's lifeless body coming back to her slung across his horse, his weather-worn ten gallon hat crushed beneath his dead weight.

Katie had been in her house stitching a quilt by candlelight when she first heard the approaching horses. Looking out of her window and seeing the posse of men, her stomach knotted into panic. Dwayne wouldn't do this to her; she hated visitors and that was a fact Dwayne was well aware of. If he was allright he would have come home to her alone, like he had promised he would. Everyone else in town was waiting for the men to return with that dead cougar but Katie wasn't one to wait around town, showing her face so people could gossip about the evil Hubbard woman. Katie knew that Dwayne longed to go into town after he and the others had killed the cougar but he had sworn he wouldn't, not wanting to evoke any more of her rage.

Katie had called her husband a fool when he had offered to help the sheriff catch the cougar. Cougars had never bothered them. They had no cattle but they had a good rifle and both of them could shoot well. Besides, neither one of them had ever seen this big, mean cat everyone was so worked up about. If it didn't affect them, why did Dwayne want to run off and waste a day looking for something he had never seen? He had told her that people were dying and he needed to go help— that was Dwayne, always trying to help somebody even if they didn't deserve it. Katie had cussed him and called him an idiot for not listening to her. Usually, if she yelled at him long enough, Dwayne could be persuaded into obeying her, but not this time. She had been reduced to begging him not to go, but that morning he had kissed her good-bye and gone. She had planned to give him a piece of her mind the second he got home, maybe even whack him with a pot, but now all she wanted was to see him come back to her with breath in his lungs. She had a bad feeling about Dwayne's whereabouts all day, and when she saw the still body slung across one of the horses, her world fell apart all around her.

Sheriff Phil approached the house cautiously, his posse following behind him in silence; even Willis had managed to tone down his tongue. Candlelight was emanating from the inside of the lonely shack; Katie was home, of course. Phil reckoned wild horses couldn't have dragged her into town for the coming home celebration. Secretly, Phil was dreading knocking on Katie's door. What was he going to say to her? Katie had a history of erratic behavior. What if, by disturbing her, he was welcoming a rifle blast at point-blank range? These worries turned out to be for nothing. Before the men could get fifty yards from the front door Katie came running out, screaming and crying, her arms outstretched and her long red hair whipping the wind behind her. Phil took a moment to consider that between the cougar, a dead man, and a wild Hubbard woman—all in one day— he was liable to finally have a nervous fit. Then Katie was standing beside Dwayne's horse, frantically shaking the body of her husband.

"Dwayne!" she wailed, panic and grief cracking her voice. "Dwayne!"

Michael, Willis, and Nick stayed as far back as they possibly could. Ron flashed Phil a what-do-we-do-now look. Remaining seated on Crow, the sheriff looked down at the hysterical woman and spoke to her in what he hoped was a soothing tone of voice.

"Katie, I'm so sorry, your husband was a good man, a brave man—"

"Murderer!" Katie screeched as she turned her fiery gaze onto the sheriff. "You killed my Dwayne!"

"Now hold on a second," Ron said. "The sheriff ain't killed nobody. A rattlesnake got Dwayne, Katie. He fell an' it bit him in the throat. It was an accident."

"Liar!" Katie spat at the deputy. "Y'all hated him 'cause he married me, a Hubbard! I'm the last of my kind here! Y'all figured that if you done murdered my husband I'd leave town or better yet, kill myself!"

"Mrs. Roberts—" Phil began, using what he hoped was an even tone of voice. In truth he was almost jumping out of his skin with worry.

"Widow Roberts!" she wailed, her grief piercing the air. "I know what y'all done. There never was no cougar. Y'all just said that to git my Dwayne to go with you so y'all could dig him his grave!"

"Look on the back of my horse," the sheriff replied patiently, gesturing toward where the cougar's carcass lay. "That there animal was as mean for blood as one could git."

"Liar!" Katie shouted again pointing to the cougar's body. "Y'all just killed that vermin to cover up your real motives—executin' my husband! Oh yes, killed him just like y'all lawmen kind have killed my uncles an' my cousins an' my brothers!"

Weeping loudly, Katie turned and began to tug on the reins of the horse carrying her husband's body. Somehow, Phil thought that Dwayne had told him once that the horse's name was Sugar. Noticing that Dwayne's hands and feet were tied together around the horse, so that his body wouldn't fall, Katie gave another little wail and attempted to undo them.

"Here, let me help you with that," Ron offered, maneuvering to dismount from his horse.

"You stay away from me!" Katie snarled. "Tell me how he's tied, and I'll set him free all by my lonesome."

"He's tied hands an' feet together, common knots," Ron replied, staying upright on Nita.

Instantly, Katie started working to untie Dwayne.

"Katie, why untie him here?" Phil asked gently. "It's easier to transport him on the horse."

"He's my husband an' I want to see him!" Katie shrieked.

Phil surrendered. Obviously logic had abandoned the situation.

Quivering, Katie untied her husband's body. The corpse was heavy and, without the securing ropes, it effortlessly slid off of the horse and fell to the ground with a sickening thud. Katie grabbed the horse and motioned it back toward the house without bothering to take off its riding gear. The horse knew where to go. Slowly it walked back toward its water and food supply.

Setting herself down on the ground, Katie cradled her husband's body in her arms as if he was a newborn baby. Softly, Katie began to sing to her dead husband, her voice was strong and pure yet hushed in the still night air. Phil couldn't tell what song she was singing but it was something sweet and comforting, like a lullaby.

"Mrs. Roberts, we need to take Dwayne's body back to town for a proper burial in the cemetery," Ron stated tentatively, deeply unnerved by Katie's antics.

"Y'all do no such thing!" Katie hissed, eyeing the deputy hatefully. "I'm buryin' my own man right here in my own yard!"

"But shouldn't he be buried in the church's grave-yard?" Ron, a man of tradition, persisted.

"Why? So local kids can come an' spit on the grave of the man who married a Hubbard? No, I have lots of land right here an' my baby is stayin' with me. I'll dig him a grave myself!"

"Well at least let us help you with that in the mornin'," Phil offered. He had deep pity for this shocked, grief-stricken woman, no matter what her family history was.

"I said I'd do it myself! Ya'll pay for what you done to my husband! I swear on my life I'll make y'all pay! Now git off my land and don't none of you come back here no more or I'll shoot a dozen holes through each of you! Go on, git out!"

Katie was openly sobbing as she screamed and pointed

her fingers away from herself. She was weak and vulnerable but she was also dangerous. Whatever was going on inside of her head was something that Phil wanted no part of. Helpless to do anything more, the sheriff honored Katie's wishes and led his remaining posse back to Dry Heat. The last vision of Katie that he saw was her small, crumpled frame on the ground, clutching her husband's body, and wailing up at the moon. Phil shivered as he rode away. He couldn't help but think, in that light, Katie looked more like a cougar than a woman.

Chapter Three

The five men rode back to Dry Heat with the morbid silence of sudden death looming like a rain cloud over their hearts and heads. As they approached the town they saw the mass of people who had been waiting all day for their return. Almost everyone was holding a lantern, thus giving the streets a warm yellow glow within the blackness of the desert night. Before the men were one hundred yards from the town the people began to cheer and didn't stop until the posse had ridden into the town's center. Phil found himself feeling a deep anger toward the townspeople as he looked at their happy faces. Did none of them notice Dwayne was missing? Did they even care? Yet those were unfair accusations. Dwayne was known to only come into town when it was absolutely necessary, so it was possible that everyone simply assumed that he was already home with Katie.

"They done killed that menace stone dead!" D.B. Gardener, the general store owner, shouted as he pointed to the dead cougar on the back of Phil's horse. Then Nick's wife, Rose, was running toward her husband screaming with relief, praising Nick for being so brave and telling him how proud she was. Nick quickly dismounted his horse so he could embrace his obviously pregnant wife.

She's mighty big in the belly, even for an expectin' woman, the sheriff thought but dismissed the idea quickly. He knew nothing about pregnant women. They were probably all that big when they got that close to birth time.

Phil was the only member of the posse still on horseback; everyone else had climbed down to embrace a loved one. Michael's wife, his mother, and his three children were gathered around him delighted that he had arrived home safely. Willis' wife was standing beside him lecturing him on scuffing his boots and dirtying his clothes—the ones she would have to wash.

Although Phil was receiving pats on the foot and "Good job pardner" comments from mostly everyone, no one in particular was waiting for him. No one had since his parents died, Clyde moved away, and Darcy drowned. Phil stopped his thoughts abruptly; he didn't want to think about Darcy, not after the long day he'd just been through.

Although Phil was left in peace to sit atop his horse and survey the scene, Ron had no such luck. Peggy Cobwey and her passive, henpecked husband, Frank, had pushed their way through the crowd to talk to the deputy—well, Peggy was talking and Frank was standing behind her as quiet as a mouse.

"Ronald!" Peggy screamed lacing her arms around Ron. "Thank the Lord you're allright! I was sure you'd be dead, eaten alive out there. I was worryin' like you don't know. I can't believe my eyes that I'm standin' here lookin' at you with all your limbs."

"That's sweet of you Mrs. Cobwey but I'm fine, really I—"

"I told Frank last night," Mrs. Cobwey continued, seeming not to have heard Ron, "I said 'Frank I just know somethin' gonna happen. I just know we gonna be buryin' Ronald.' Didn't I, Frank?"

Frank nodded.

"See? I told you I said them things an' thank the Lord I was wrong." Standing back she observed Ron with a worried eye. "You look flushed. Did you get heat stroke? Was that beef I fixed for you last night okay? Are you crampin'?"

"I'm fine, Mrs. Cobwey," Ron replied, suppressing a grin. When his mother died from yellow fever when he was seven, Peggy Cobwey had become a sort of surrogate mother to him. She had no children of her own, and she treated Ron as if he were her own flesh and blood. Furthermore, Mrs. Cobwey had become a nurse to Ron's father, Dan. Already in his forties when Ron was born, Dan had fallen into a deeply confused solitude after the death of his wife, an ailment which only got worse as time went on.

Phil watched everyone else mingle and chatter from the top of his horse. He could tell that folks were relieved to see their loved ones again and the cougar dead. Although he hated to put an end to the good cheer, he decided that it was time to tell the townsfolk what had happened to Dwayne. Somehow it didn't seem right to celebrate when a good young man was lying dead.

"Everyone!" Phil shouted loudly, but his voice was quickly lost amid the general noise of the crowd. "I need y'all attention!" he screamed louder, still to no avail. So much for being the man in charge. The sheriff looked down at the pistol strapped to his side. *Shoot one of 'em bullets into the air an' I'd get all eyes on me mighty fast.* But he quickly dismissed the notion. Phil used to be good with a gun, but after years behind a desk with little cause to use it, he'd resigned himself to utilizing his weapon only as a last resort.

"Hear, Hear!" a gruff voice suddenly boomed from the back of the crowd. The sound was loud and echoing; its vibrations shook the ground as if a small earthquake was in progress. Laying a comforting hand on Crow, who was nervous around loud noises, Phil looked toward the voice and saw Larry Tulmacher pushing his way through the crowd. Larry was an enormous man in girth; he spanned what normally would have been the space of two or three men. The second Larry spoke the crowd turned to look at him. *There's a man who has no trouble bein' heard,* Phil thought, feeling inadequate.

Larry and his band of rough-shaven, hard-drinking, fast-fisted, and shifty-eyed cohorts had ridden into Dry Heat about a year ago. They were from the South which was, as Larry always said with a note of sadness in his voice, still in a state of wreckage from the Civil War. Immediately after arriving in Dry Heat, Larry started preaching all the reasons why the town needed a leader, someone to look out for the people—a mayor. It was really no wonder that the townspeople had been persuaded to feel that Larry would make a good mayor. Don Rombert, the current mayor of Dry Heat, was an alcoholic. He was so wrapped up in his whiskey and rum that he hadn't even bothered to sober up for tonight's greeting party. Phil reckoned the mayor was still passed out in his office, completely unaware of cougar hunts or political competition.

Don was wifeless and childless. He was the last descendant in a three-generation line of Dry Heat mayors, going back to when the town had first been established. Noting that Don had no children, was a hopeless alcoholic, and was getting on in years, it was only logical for the townspeople to start thinking about electing a future mayor—someone of a new bloodline who was clever and full of new ideas. Larry fit that mold.

Although he never made his suspicions known, the sheriff felt that there was something shady about Larry, something wrong. Larry seemed to be more of a con artist than a politician and his interests were more to-ward himself than anyone else. Like how he talked his way into renting six rooms above Claire's Cactus for himself and his crew free of charge, or the way he con-stantly connived free drinks out of the bartender. He ranted and raved about righteousness yet he spent most of his time in Claire's Cactus drinking whiskey and pinching barmaids' bottoms. The thing that Phil found the most troubling about Larry was how arrogant he was during his speeches. Everything from his education to his once-wealthy, pre-war Southern lifestyle was end-lessly boasted about. Of course the townspeople believed every word he said, including his insistence that their European ancestry was to be praised and guarded. The people of Dry Heat were sheltered and gullible and, therefore, quick to listen to Larry who presented himself as an educated, wealthy, and worldly man.

Watching Larry and his cohorts push through the crowd, making their way toward him, Phil eyed Clarence Harden, the preacher's nephew, following be-hind the politician. Although the short, skinny, beady-eyed Clarence looked even smaller than usual behind Larry, he walked with the same air of self–entitled ar-rogance that Phil had pegged as a Clarence Harden trait years before. Some things never changed.

Clarence had started hanging around Larry and his cohorts the same week they had come to town. Clarence wasn't exactly the most beloved young man in Dry Heat; in fact, he was almost universally disliked. Clarence was, and had always been, a mean-spirited troublemaker who was constantly being defended by his preacher uncle. Clarence had been orphaned as a young child after his parents died in a fire. Warren had taken his nephew in and doted on the boy, who had been high-spirited even at the age of six. Warren didn't have the heart to discipline Clarence, and the boy took advantage of his uncle's weakness. Often, Phil found himself feeling deep pity for the preacher. Warren was a kind man who loved his nephew and wished to raise him right, yet he had absolutely no control over the boy's actions. What was worse, every time Clarence did something wrong, the preacher would come to his nephew's defense. Not that Clarence ever did anything really bad—illegally bad. Oh no, Clarence was crooked and ugly in spirit, but in speech and on paper he was as proper and righteous as his uncle. Still, it was hushed knowledge around town that, at the age of twenty-three, Clarence was just as out of control as he had been when he was six.

Phil had an acute dislike for Clarence. The sheriff reckoned that his poor opinion of the fellow began three years ago when Clarence decided that he wanted to be the town jailer. Normally, Phil or Ron looked after any prisoners they had in the town's lone jail cell. For the most part, the people put in the cell were drunken cowboys who needed some time to sober up. Although Phil had no real need or desire for a jailer, the preacher thought a job would do his lackluster nephew a world of good and he begged the sheriff to give Clarence the position. After a month of listening to the preacher's endless pleas, Phil gave in and awarded Clarence the job. At

the time, Phil had seen no harm in this action. He figured
that Clarence would end up sitting around an empty jail
all day picking his nose. Back then Phil had no way to
know that he was unleashing one of the most chaotic situations which would ever plague Dry Heat.

A little over six months after Clarence had been appointed town jailer, the sheriff and the deputy had the
good fortune of capturing Bernie "Blackeye" Crawdrum. Blackeye was a murdering bandit who had ter-
rorized small desert towns far and wide. Cattle Skull, a
town about thirty miles east of Dry Heat, was the last
place Blackeye had robbed. Phil personally knew Sheriff Andy McDowde of Cattle Skull; in fact, the two men
had been friends before they were old enough to shave.
Directly after Blackeye was placed in the Dry Heat jail,
Phil had sent Hugh Gardener, the son of the general
store owner, to Cattle Skull to inform Sheriff McDowde
of Blackeye's capture. In normal circumstances either
Ron or Phil would have stood guard over the cell con-
taining Blackeye, but Blackeye was no average criminal. Word of mouth spreads fast in small towns and word
of Blackeye's capture had spread like wild fire around
Dry Heat. Less than an hour after Blackeye was sitting
in his cell, the townspeople demanded that the sheriff
give a speech about what was going to be done with
the bandit. Phil had reckoned that the criminal would
be hanged, but he wasn't too keen on giving a speech to
state this idea. Phil was a quiet-enough man who was
nervous about speaking in front of large crowds, and
when he got nervous he stuttered. Ron was much better

at running his mouth off, so the sheriff had forced the deputy to stand beside him as he made his speech. Phil figured that the younger man could speak for him if he froze up. At the time Phil had thought that stuttering like a fool in public was the worst of his worries. Neither he nor Ron thought twice about leaving Clarence to guard Blackeye, who was locked tightly inside the prison.

The speech had lasted a while but it had gone well; the return to the jailhouse had not. Upon returning, Phil and Ron discovered a gagged and tied Clarence lying on the floor under the sheriff's desk. Across the room stood an empty jail cell, the unlocked door standing ajar. The news of Blackeye's escape caused a panic in the town. Every rancher and cowpoke within a twenty-mile radius had searched the desert for the bandit but all the effort equaled no success. According to Clarence, the criminal had been gone for over an hour and had taken his horse with him. Blackeye had probably been miles away before the sheriff had even known about his escape. If it was hard to tell the Dry Heat townsfolk about the escape of Blackeye, it had been ten times harder to tell Sheriff McDowde. When Sheriff McDowde arrived in Dry Heat and heard the news, he threw his hat onto the desert dust and cussed Phil for being so careless in the keeping of prisoners.

Clarence insisted that Blackeye had gotten out of the cell because Ron had failed to lock the cell correctly, but Phil knew that was a lie. He had watched Ron lock Blackeye in and the deputy had done a secure job.

Something else had been going on in that jailhouse in order for Blackeye to have escaped—something either stupid or corrupt, the two things Clarence feared being exposed as. Phil had tried to pry the truth out of Clarence more times than he could count, but the boy was a sneaky good liar who knew how to keep a secret.

Most of the town blamed Clarence for letting Blackeye escape, and they weren't shy about openly scorning him. Clarence had eventually started spending all his time on his uncle's ranch behind the chapel. The preacher said that his nephew was taking some spiritual time to connect to God and absorb knowledge. Phil knew that was just the preacher's way of saying that Clarence had been humiliated into secrecy. For over a year and a half no one saw much of Clarence, and Phil had started to believe that the young man would become a lifelong hermit. Then Larry and his men came to town, and Clarence emerged from his solitude, once again becoming the self-righteous and obnoxious presence he always had been in Dry Heat.

"Darn good huntin' there, fellas!" Larry shouted at Phil in an overly pleasant voice, which immediately snapped the sheriff away from his thoughts. "Yes sir-ree, some fine shootin' been done there, Palmer!"

The sheriff forced a smile. For some reason the politician insisted on calling him by his last name. Not a fan of being addressed by his surname, Phil had asked Larry several times to call him simply Phil or Sheriff but Larry seemed to lack the ability to do so. Ron said that he had once overheard Larry claim that back in the

Confederate Army everyone was called by their last name and, after all the years he had spent there, the habit stuck. Nevertheless, Phil found the quirk unbearably annoying and old fashioned. It was 1871, the war had ended in 1865.

"I'll say, Palmer," Larry said with a chuckle as he stood beside the sheriff's horse and looked up at the dead cougar. "You and the five men with you are brave—"

"Four men."

"Pardon?"

"Only four men came back with me," Phil announced loudly. Finally he had the attention of the crowd. All eyes were on him and he could feel the unease of public speaking creeping up his spine. "We lost Dwayne Roberts during the trip."

"How?" Larry asked as a chorus of gasps and murmurs arose around him.

"We was comin' down the mountains after killin' the cougar an' Dwayne tripped an' got himself bitten by a rattlesnake. He died within minutes. We dropped his body off with his wife."

"But he'll need a churchyard burial!" the politician cried, always taking time to convey himself as a deeply pious man.

"Not accordin' to his widow. She's buryin' him out on her land, and she don't want no help doin' it neither. I pity the soul who tries to defy her. You know how she is about folks treadin' on her property."

"Good people of Dry Heat, a tragedy has befallen us!" Larry turned and shouted at the crowd dramatically. "Yes

Lord, the tragedy of the death of a man hardly more than a youngin'! Let us all have a moment of silence to remember this young man an' all he done for this town in his short life!"

The politician bowed his head and the rest of Dry Heat followed his lead. Phil, still perched on top of Crow, watched the scene uneasily. It was unnerving how much control Larry had over the townspeople. Even after the moment of silence had passed, the mood of the town was tense and awkward. The festive spirits of five minutes ago had died into a dull quiet. Unsurprisingly, Willis broke the silence: "Well, at least we got the cougar."

Sounds of agreement rose in the crowd as a wave of rage rose inside of Phil. Dwayne was dead, probably without as much as a prayer service, and a moment of silence was all the remembrance he got before celebration arose once again? Maybe Katie was right, maybe Dwayne having married a Hubbard did make him worthless according to most of the folks around Dry Heat.

"The man is correct!" Larry boomed, pointing at Willis. All the former sorrow was gone from his voice and he seemed delighted to have a way to lift the mood. "Our loss was great but our victory was greater! I say we're all entitled to celebrate this accomplishment at Claire's Cactus!"

The crowd cheered as Phil tried to keep himself steady on his horse. Was celebrating at Claire's Cactus how the town would have reacted if *he* had died? Although everyone else in his posse was putting their horses in the big corral behind the sheriff's office and surging toward the bar with the rest of the town, Phil stayed put on his horse. He reckoned he'd wait until everyone was gone, dismount, and get an early night's sleep. Feeling a sudden tap on his foot, Phil looked down and saw Ron.

"Come on, pardner, have a drink on me."

"Y'all go, I ain't thirsty."

"No," Ron replied firmly, "you come too. It's been a long day. You had no control over what happened to Dwayne. You did all you could for him. Come have a drink, it'll do you good."

Normally the sheriff would have ignored the younger man's suggestion, but tonight Phil reckoned Ron was right. He did need to rest and, despite what he had claimed, he was thirsty for either a glass of water or a whole gallon of whiskey. After dismounting Crow and settling the horse into the corral with the others, Phil allowed himself to be led into the town saloon.

Chapter Four

Claire's Cactus was a rickety, wooden-walled, and dirt-floored saloon decorated with furniture that shook and a stage that creaked. Plays and dances were performed on the stage a few nights a week, but that was the height of culture at Claire's Cactus. Strings, a guitar-playing wino, was sitting in his usual corner watching as people surged into the bar. Strings was, in many ways, the perfect representation of the type of folks who normally came to Claire's Cactus. The general clientele was drifters and cowboys. The barmaids, with their tight, low-cut clothes and cozy upstairs rooms could almost always be bought for a price. Phil had no idea how much a man would have to pay for the attention of one of the saloon girls. He wasn't a man who fell for that sort of woman. Heck, he'd never fallen for any woman except Darcy . . .

A barmaid rammed into a chair, knocking it to the floor. The sharp sound of the chair connecting to the dirt ground jolted Phil out of his thoughts. How he had managed to drift into thought in the middle of Claire's Cactus, he couldn't understand. One glance at the action inside of the room was enough to strain his eyes. Claire's Cactus was packed with people, some of whom looked comically out of place.

Wendy Philips, Dry Heat's prim schoolteacher, was standing just within the barroom doorway. A woman with a flawlessly proper reputation, Wendy seemed utterly horrified to be seen in Claire's Cactus. Every time a barmaid scurried by in a revealing outfit, Wendy mouthed a small "Lord save us." The vision made Phil, who had always been good at reading lips, smile. Sure, now Wendy was acting outraged, but once she got a few sips of whiskey into her she'd be up at the front of the saloon draped over the piano and singing her heart out. He had heard Wendy sing before and, being a fan of her raw yet smooth voice, he hoped someone would give her a whiskey soon.

The sheriff and the deputy seated themselves at a small, rickety table in a corner. Instantly they were approached by a young, dark-haired, and light-eyed barmaid. Phil recognized her as Carrie Halod whom Deputy Ron had his eyes and heart set on for almost two years. From the way he stared at the slim barmaid, Ron's crush was obvious.

All the sheriff knew about Carrie was that she arrived in Dry Heat by train about two years ago. She had come with nothing to her name but a few worn house dresses, a battered suitcase, and shoes so old they had holes in them. She had quickly taken up work at the saloon, mainly because the bar had a stage and Carrie yearned to be an actress. She was provided with a room upstairs, and she was paid and fed every day. The downside, of course, was that Claire's Cactus was half a brothel, and Carrie wasn't the type of girl who was fond of drunken cowboys.

Carrie came back to the table and quickly set down the sheriff's and deputy's drinks. Then, without a word or a glance, she headed over to another part of the crowded bar. Ron's eyes followed her until she was out of sight.

Darn fool is just lookin' to go fallin' in love. Stupid, hateful emotion; he'll regret it one day. Ever since losing Darcy, reminders of romance caused Phil a pang of pain.

Three women suddenly approached the table, surrounding Ron. Their presence brought the sheriff out of his thoughts. Unsurprisingly, the deputy's female visitors were the three Doherty women—the widow, Adeline, and her two daughters, Edwina and Amelia. For the past couple of years the younger Doherty women had been pursuing Ron as a husband and the elder Doherty woman had been looking to make him her son-in-law.

Adeline Doherty was a large, dull-haired yet fiery-eyed woman. She stood at medium height but she had a way of standing right up in front of a person, thus making herself seem far taller than she was. Her demeanor was curt, her voice was screechy, and her requests were demanding.

Her eldest daughter, Edwina, was a chunky girl who was known for being extremely prudish. Furthermore, although she was certainly no beauty, Edwina was as vain as could be. Although she was only seventeen years old, Edwina often acted like a woman three times her age.

Fifteen-year-old Amelia was as pushy as her mother but the polar opposite of her prudish sister. Amelia liked to get attention, particularly the attention of young men, and she wasn't shy about displaying her body to secure that which she yearned for. Out of the three Dohertys, Amelia was the slimmest and prettiest. She took after her daddy, Ed, who had been killed in a wagon accident when she was no more than a year old. Yet, although Amelia was pretty, she had meanness about her, a glint in her eye which made her keen on looking for, and often finding, trouble.

"Oh my God, Deputy Ronald Harris, you had us so worried!" Adeline screeched as she stood before Ron, her hands on her hips and a cross look on her face.

She looks like an angry vulture, Phil thought but dared not say.

"'Course its terrible what happened to that Dwayne fella, but thank the Lord it wasn't you! Why, my girls couldn't hardly stand it! They was darn near in tears. Amelia was so wild with fear she was angry. You should see her when she's mad! She told me if that cougar laid a paw on you she'd git her daddy's old gun and shoot every cougar around these parts stone dead."

"An' I meant that. I'd do anythin' for you, Ron," the youngest Doherty daughter crooned as she pushed herself halfway over the table to bat her eyes at the deputy.

"That's mighty sweet of you, miss," Ron replied for the sake of being polite. In truth he didn't think there was anything sweet about any of the Doherty women.

Still standing close enough to the seated deputy to make herself look like a giant, Adeline launched into one of her long speeches about the many virtues of her daughters, but Ron didn't hear a word she said. Carrie was back in view over at the bar. She was handing out bottles of whiskey and forcing herself to smile. Carrie was a good sort, the kind of girl Ron could see himself sitting down with and talking to about mostly anything without feeling uneasy. She was a good listener, but what was he supposed to say to her? She was a woman who could act on stage as if she was somebody else and make the audience believe her. How was he expected to speak to such an amazing person? How—

"Ronald, I reckon your mind is over one thousand miles away from me," Adeline snapped harshly, diverting the deputy's eyes away from Carrie.

"Sorry, ma'am, it's been a long day," Ron replied, flashing what he hoped was his best, most apologetic smile.

"He was lookin' at that Carrie harlot!" Edwina hissed.

"Edwina, don't say that word!" Adeline scolded.

"Why not? If she wasn't then why's she workin' here?"

"I don't know what you see in her!" Amelia spat at Ron. "Don't you think there's better lookin' women 'round this town?"

"Now that you mention it, not many," Ron retorted, greatly enjoying the look of outrage on the Dohertys' faces. *Family's judgin' Carrie an' their own gonna be workin' the tables in here real soon,* he thought, taking notice of the way Amelia turned her body seductively toward him as she questioned him. Even as he fought to keep himself in control around the Dohertys, Ron was unable to fully take his eyes off of Carrie. This clearly annoyed Adeline.

"You know, Ronald," Adeline began, squinting her eyes and fixing the deputy with a scolding gaze, "you're not gettin' any younger, an' sooner or later you're gonna need to find yourself a wife. Start thinkin' about the kind of woman you wanna have momma your babies. Now come on girls, let's go say hello to the future Mayor Tulmacher and his friends—such sweet men!"

Adeline turned away from the deputy and the sheriff and ushered her girls away from their table. Phil watched the Doherty women as they spoke to Larry and his cohorts on the other side of the room. Amelia seemed absolutely delighted by all the winks and nods the rough-looking men in the politician's gang gave her.

"Looks like you've chased your lady friends off," Phil joked to Ron.

"All them vermin deserve each other," Ron snarled as he eyed the Dohertys and the politician contemptuously.

The sound of tinkling piano keys directed all eyes toward the back left-hand corner. Claire, the plump, middle-aged, and over-rouged owner of the saloon, was sitting at the piano, and Strings was poised near her ready to play his guitar. A very flushed-looking Wendy Philips was standing beside Strings, leaning back against the piano, holding a glass of whiskey in her right hand, ready to sing.

"She started early," Ron stated, not trying to hide his smirk.

"Her voice ain't nowhere near bad once she let's herself sing though," Phil replied and settled back into his chair. He was looking forward to hearing the schoolteacher's sweet, rich voice. Wendy was usually soft spoken and pushy but when she sang she was strong-voiced and sweet. Tonight she was singing some old gospel hymn which guided her voice into both high and low pitches.

"You hear all that talk about a dust storm blowin' in?" Ron shouted over the music.

"No," the sheriff shouted back, straining to hear.

"I heard a couple of old fellas talkin', sayin' that a good-sized dust storm is due to hit us real soon."

"Is that so?"

"Accordin' to the elders."

"Elders can be wrong. They git confused."

"About storms? When's the last time an old-timer was wrong about the weather? The last couple of times the elders predicted a storm it came within a week an' it hit real hard. We lost more than a few cattle that way. If they say there's gonna be a storm, then I'm inclined to believe 'em."

"Well, that's just perfect then," Phil replied and spat onto the floor, "just one problem after another."

"Ain't it the truth," the deputy replied and sighed. "We should prepare though, just in case it's ugly."

"You ever feel like the whole world's gone ugly?"

"What do you mean?"

"Crazed cougars, rattlesnakes, accidental deaths, politicians, storms—everythin' hittin' this town."

"You forgot about angry Indians," the deputy replied, grinning.

"Them too. All hot tempered toward us for livin' on the land an' diggin' in them mines, only gonna get worse now that they say gold is in them creeks by us. An' I've heard that further west there's even more gold, more than can be counted."

The sheriff and the deputy grew silent listening to Wendy's voice filter through the saloon. It had been a long, hard, and sorrowful day, and the mere idea of harder ones to come weighed down on the sheriff's mind like a boulder. Fighting a headache, Phil leaned back in his chair, closed his eyes, and let the music engulf him.

What the sheriff didn't know was that angry Indians and dust storms were the least of his worries. Late that night, as everyone in Dry Heat slept soundly in their beds, Katie Hubbard sneaked around the back of Phil's office.

She had finished burying Dwayne an hour beforehand and she had left her home as soon as her husband was in the ground. Her few traveling items were packed and secured onto Sugar's saddle, all except for her daddy's old pistol which she kept in his old gunbelt around her waist.

Katie knew what the townspeople were up to. They had been at the bar all night celebrating the death of Dwayne. They hated her and they had killed Dwayne to spite her and chase her out of town like they had done to the rest of her kin. They had wanted to run her out of town for years, and they had decided to kill Dwayne to speed up the process. They had thought they'd get away with it, but they were wrong. Katie was going to make them pay for what they had done. Sure, she'd leave town for now but she'd be back, oh yes-sir-ree, she would indeed.

Katie knew where her family had moved to and she knew how to get there. Amanda, her favorite sister, had secretly told her all of the details of the Hubbard family's moving plan before they had left. In times like these Katie was angry that she could neither read nor write— sending a letter would be simple if she only possessed those two skills. Yet, since she was not skilled with the written word, her horse and her memory would just have to do to get her back to her family. But first she would give the town of Dry Heat a little going away present.

Behind the jailhouse was a large corral where most of the townspeople left their horses at night. Katie reckoned that the corral was built there because thieves—like her family—would be wary about stealing a horse from under a sheriff's nose.

Tonight there were about twenty horses sleeping in the corral. Working quickly and silently, Katie opened the corral gate without dismounting Sugar. Once the door was fully open, Katie positioned herself on Sugar. She expected to ride away from the scene as fast as possible.

Looking up at the sky, Katie envisioned her husband's sweet face. Allowing a single tear to fall, she pulled the pistol out of the gunbelt, pointed it toward the sky, and pulled the trigger.

The blast was a loud explosion of light amid the silent darkness of the night. As she expected, the noise and the flash startled the horses in the corral badly. Panicked, they began to run. A small buckskin was the first horse to run out of the open corral. The other horses followed, Crow and Nita among them. The animals stampeded away in panic, causing the earth to vibrate.

The townspeople were awakened by the commotion. Katie saw lanterns being lit and sleepy townsfolk stumbling out of their homes. She thought she saw Phil Palmer, clad in his undergarments, run out of the sheriff's quarters cussing and swearing as he eyed the horses running off into the desert.

Sugar had also been frightened by the pistol blast. Seconds after firing the gun, Katie found herself riding quickly out to the desert, laughing manically, heading fifty miles east to rejoin her kin and seek her revenge.

Chapter Five

Rounding up the horses was not an easy task. Phil, Ron, and every other able-bodied man from town had been out on the plains since sunrise attempting to retrieve the escaped horses. Most of the animals had tired of running after about a mile and had simply stopped and stood in the desert waiting for someone to lead them back to town. The majority—Crow and Nita among them—were rounded up early in the morning and brought back to Dry Heat for food, water, and rest. Phil thanked his lucky stars that the ranchers and cowpokes around the outskirts of town didn't leave their horses in the main corral. If it hadn't been for a few men on horseback with good roping skills, half the escaped horses would not have been returned to safety.

It was approaching noon. The sun shone mercilessly, baking the earth and cruelly mocking the men under its rays—most of whom were ready to pass out from ex-haustion. Yet there was still a fair bit of work to be done. Lloyd, Willis Lauder's horse, was running rampant from the men. Still irked from the events of the night before, the pinto was resisting rescue by running ten feet away from anyone who took one step toward him. A handful of cowpokes on horseback were trying to rope Lloyd as a dozen men on foot attempted to form a barrier around the animal. All the men were cussing with frustration, exhaustion, and annoyance.

It's like lookin' at organized chaos, Phil thought and spat onto the ground. He had never been so exhausted in his life. Aside from running after the escaped horses, he had been up extra early to bury the corpse of the cougar deep in the ground—it was the only way to ensure that no other animals would eat its body and get the same disease.

The sheriff was trying to control his temper but it was a difficult task, especially when he thought about Katie. He had tried to be compassionate to her. He had tried to be courteous. He and his posse had brought Dwayne back to her and told her the news before any-one else. They had offered to give him a proper burial and would have brought her into town to witness it. Phil had done his best but Katie had handled his attempts of empathy and compassion by releasing more than half of the town's horses into the wild where the domesti-cated animals could be hurt or killed. He suspected that Katie was behind this mischief from the second he heard the gunshot, which had roused him from his slumber. His suspicions were confirmed at daybreak when he and Ron had gone out to pay Katie a visit and found her house abandoned; Dwayne's grave still fresh behind the shack.

Phil reckoned that Dwayne was spinning in his grave seeing what his wife had done to the townspeople he had grown so fond of. To make matters worse, Katie had used horses to justify her crazy rage: horses, the animals Dwayne loved most. Although most of the horses were safe, Lloyd was still on the loose and five others were missing altogether.

It's just like a Hubbard to turn kindness into evil plots, the sheriff thought angrily. *We're lucky she didn't burn the whole dang town to the ground. I reckon she'd be crazy enough to do it if she'd thought of it.*

"Dang it, Lloyd, git your carcass back here!" Willis suddenly shrieked, running on foot and shaking his fist at his horse.

"You ain't gonna catch him that way; heck, you'll chase him straight over to Mad Maggie's first!" one cowpoke informed the banker, instigating a howl of laughter from the other men.

Mad Maggie—there was a name the sheriff hadn't heard in a while, probably because he hadn't seen the lady in question in quite some time. Mad Maggie was a middle-aged woman who lived somewhere on the other side of the coal mines. She had no known friends or family, and Phil wasn't aware of her having any sort of job. She was a running joke among the townspeople—the town misfit whom older children claimed was a witch to frighten younger children. Personally, Phil never saw any reason to be particularly interested in Maggie. She didn't come into town often but whenever she did she seemed like a friendly enough type. She wore aging dresses which had been sewn just well enough to look proper. She was reclusive, yet not troublesome, and that made the townspeople wary of her yet not disdainful. Phil had no idea how long Maggie had lived near the town, although her coal-black hair was turning gray, so he reckoned she was close to his own age, maybe a few years older. One way or another, Maggie had never done, or been accused of doing, anything that needed the sheriff paying a visit to her home. Mad or not, she was no troublemaker.

"Poor critters," Ron declared, walking to Phil's side and startling him out of his thoughts. "She really scared the life out of 'em." The deputy had been watching the capturing of the horses all day with great pity. He was a horseman at heart and hated to see the animals in such a state of agitation.

"We'll get as many as we can," Phil replied. "We'll tire Lloyd out an' get him on back to town. Then we'll take some of the better rested horses and ride around lookin' for the five that have gone missin'."

"Sounds like a plan," Ron remarked, never taking his eyes off of Lloyd.

"This is all because of Katie," Phil spat. "I swear, if there ever was a woman who deserved hangin'—"

A trembling under his feet made Phil stop speaking. A steady vibration was rocking the earth from far off in the distance, almost as if lightning was hitting the ground. Yet the sky was blue and cloudless—this was no lightning storm.

"What do you hear?" Ron asked, noting the sheriff's still posture.

"Do you feel that?"

"Feel what?"

"Ground's movin', slightly, but its sure shakin'."

"'Course it's shakin'. Lloyd an' all them fellas after him are just a few feet away."

"This ain't Lloyd; the ground didn't feel like this a few minutes ago."

Both men stood watching the horizon. Phil had been born with a good sense of hearing; if he thought something was coming he was probably right. Yet it was impossible to hear anything over the sound of Lloyd, Willis, and the other men. Ron suggested telling them to hush up, but Phil refused the idea. He didn't want to risk seeming foolish. He had been under stress and it was possible that the ground shaking really was from Lloyd, and the sinking feeling in his stomach was due to little sleep and too much hard work. Maybe, hopefully, it *was* all in his head. Yet, the longer they stood, the stronger the vibrations in the ground got—something was coming all right. This was not the sheriff's imagination.

The sun was intense. Its bright rays beat upon the red desert sand forming mirages in the distance and giving the impression that a river was flowing along the ground. Phil cussed the sun's tricks; it was impossible to see what was coming with the mirage hovering on the horizon. It was a good three minutes before he saw the outline of a dozen approaching Indians. They were riding hard, hollering war cries, and brandishing weapons.

Apaches, Phil thought as a shiver climbed down his spine.

As far back as Phil could remember, towns like Dry Heat had experienced unpleasant confrontations with Apache Indians. He supposed that he couldn't blame them for disliking whites. After all, the vast land that had once been theirs had been taken via betrayal and brutality, leaving nothing but a trail of tears and blood. Often Phil felt great sympathy for the native people, but he also harvested a deep fear of them. Their rage, their warriors, their weapons, and their scalpings were enough to make any man weak with stone-cold fear.

"Injuns!" Ron shrieked, finding his voice before Phil found his. Hearing Ron's cry, the other men looked up, saw the approaching Indians, and ran for cover behind tall cactus and boulders. Guns were loaded and cocked as the men took shelter. Lloyd, frightened by the sudden movements and shaking ground, darted away until his wide frame was nothing more than a tiny speck.

An arrow flew through the air and struck Hugh Gardener right through the shoulder. Hugh hit the ground with a thud and lay screaming in agony. Nick Stooker grabbed and dragged the wounded man behind a boulder for cover. The first arrow led to the swift launch of others. The townsmen returned fire with their rifles and pistols.

For Phil, the Indian attack resembled being back in the cave with the cougar—everything happened so fast that he felt dizzy. The Apaches, who had been visions in the distance moments before, were now riding through the center of the horse-searching party. As always when he fought, Phil's mind went into overdrive. Whenever he was in a dangerous situation that called for the use of his gun, Phil's mind became focused and connected to his weapon. In times of battle nothing in the world mattered aside from himself and his gun.

From behind a cactus, Phil was aiming and shooting without really thinking, turning his body around agilely so he could protect all sides of him. He wasn't sure if he was aiming well or hitting any targets because it was so difficult to see what was happening. A thick blanket of dusty sand mixed with gunpowder smoke was blowing in every direction, stinging eyes and filling nostrils. The air was filled with the sounds of Indian war cries, screams of pain, gunshots, and frightened horses. Under his surface numbness and disconnection, the sheriff was scared silly. Dwayne died yesterday, the majority of men from town were out here now, and he couldn't see any of them. How many men would Dry Heat lose today?

From behind him, Phil heard horse hooves. He turned swiftly and saw an Apache coming towards him. The Indian was pointing an arrow at the sheriff. Immediately, Phil aimed and pulled the trigger of his pistol. The shot was perfectly executed. The Indian's cry went from rage to pain, his face from anger to surprise. He fell forward on his horse, dropping his shield and releasing the arrow harmlessly into the air.

Arrows were falling from the sky like rain, and bullets were being fired from every direction. Then, as quickly as it had started, it was over. The Apaches, realizing how vastly outnumbered they were, rode away still hollering war cries and waving their weapons angrily.

Phil waited for the dust to clear before emerging from behind the cactus. Relief encased him when he saw a shaken but unharmed Ron standing a few feet away. The young deputy was like a son and he couldn't stomach the thought of the younger man getting hurt or worse.

"What in the name of Abraham Lincoln brought that on?" Willis screeched, looking like he was ready to cry.

"Old animosities, Will," the sheriff replied before turning toward the deputy. "How many are dead an' how many are wounded?"

"We got lucky," the deputy replied. "Nobody's dead, but Hugh here is gonna need a doctor mighty soon."

It was true; Hugh had the arrow stuck deeply in his shoulder, his face was drained of color, and the wound was seeping blood. The sheriff didn't know which thought was worse—the process of removing the arrow or the illness that would set in if it was left lodged in the skin. Fighting a wave of nausea, Phil thanked God he wasn't in Hugh's place.

"It's amazin' none of us got ourselves killed," Ron declared. Phil had to agree with him. It certainly was incredible that after that entire attack the worst injury their party had suffered was an arrow to the shoulder.

"How many Injuns we get?" Willis demanded to know.

"I ain't sure we killed any, no bodies here anyway, but I think about three were shot," Ron replied.

"It's about two miles back to town. Are you up to ridin' back on a horse, Hugh?" Phil asked.

"Can't we get a stretcher to pull him on?" Ron asked.

"I'm afraid by the time we get there an' back he'll have lost half his blood."

"It's okay," Hugh replied grimacing, "I can make it back. It hurts bad but I can't stay here."

"Brave man," Phil replied, "I'd give you a ride myself but my horse is back in town restin' up."

As Hugh was helped up to a rancher's horse, Phil turned to the rest of the men and declared the horse search over.

"But what about Lloyd?" Willis squawked.

That's a good question, Phil thought but did not say. Horses were herding animals, and if he had followed the Apaches horses, then he was already under Indian ownership. Phil knew that after the day's events the chances of catching any of the missing horses was too slight to exhaust his men over. In truth, the sheriff doubted if any of the missing horses would ever be seen again. Still, it didn't seem right to say something like that to Willis. In times like these rubbing the truth in wasn't going to do anyone any good.

"We'll leave some food outside the corral for him,"

Phil explained. "If he comes back he'll be able to eat and then we'll rope him an' put him back in with the others."

"But won't leavin' food out like that attract cougars an' pumas an' other things that can go hurtin' a horse?" Willis retorted, sounding horrified.

"Cougars an' pumas like meat; they ain't got no interest in oats and hay."

"I know that! But what if they come after him? He's meat, ain't he?"

"He can probably outrun anythin' lookin' to hurt him out on the range an' if he comes back into town he's safe. I ain't never heard of no pumas or cougars comin' into a town to hunt."

"But what if he's already hurt?" Willis declared dramatically. "What if he got an arrow stuck in him or what if he fell an' hurt his leg?"

The sheriff had to admit that, for all of Willis' faults, the banker really did care about his horse. Phil reckoned he'd be just as nervous if it was Crow who had gone missing. Willis' fears were more than justifiable, and Phil thought the man deserved some sort of consolation.

"Willis," Phil began kindly, "we're doin' all we can. If you want to you can stay up tonight an' keep on the lookout in case Lloyd comes back. I could even fix it to hire some cowpokes to help you but horses don't travel much at night—your best bet is lookin' again tomorrow."

"I know," Willis replied gazing at the desert floor, his hands buried deep inside his pants pockets and a frown on his face, "I just wish I hadn't been yellin' at him before."

I hope that horse comes back. He's got a good owner in Willis.

Phil began the trek back to town, watching as the injured Hugh and the ranch hand galloped away. They were already yards ahead of the sheriff and the other walking men. It felt strange to travel the desert on foot. Phil couldn't remember the last time he had been without Crow during a journey of any great distance. Still, he was glad the horse had been taken back to town early on in the day to get food and water. He was also thankful that Crow hadn't been around during the Indian attack. Phil often worried about Crow being fatally wounded in a gunfight. It was funny how much a horse could grow on an owner. The sheriff felt a sudden pang of deep sympathy for Willis. He had no way of knowing what had become of his horse and chances were that he never would.

Thank God I ain't in his shoes. The first thing I'm gonna do when I get into town is give Crow a big pat an' tell him how glad I am that he ain't out wanderin' the desert aimlessly. The thought made the sheriff smile; if anyone heard him out in the corral talking to his horse, they would reckon he'd lost his mind. Still, that didn't seem so bad in comparison to the past two days.

Phil kept referring back to Katie and, whenever he thought about her, rage boiled up inside of him. It was because of her that Lloyd and five other horses were missing. It was because of her that the Apaches had a chance to attack the townsmen. It was because of her that Hugh Gardener was injured. It was because of her that Phil had been forced to shoot a man. Self defense or not, the idea that he had most likely ended another human being's life bothered the sheriff a great deal.

"Curse that woman," Phil muttered. He had never been so weary nor had he ever experienced such a chaotic two days and, truth be told, a great many of his problems had been caused by the Hubbard woman. As he walked back to town Phil prayed that he would never lay eyes on Katie again.

A deeper instinct told him that was one prayer which wouldn't be answered.

Chapter Six

"Well, today was just another sweet stroll through the flower patch," Phil declared sarcastically as he sipped his whiskey.

"At least nobody was killed," Ron replied, slouching in his chair.

"None of us townsfolk at least, but I think I got that Indian good. I reckon I killed him. Dang fool thing for them to have done, attackin' us like that."

"It was pure self defense on your part."

"I know that but it don't mean I like the facts any better."

It was just past nightfall. The sheriff and the deputy were unwinding in Claire's Cactus. Right outside the building a pail of oats and a pail of water had been set out in case any horses returned during the night. Willis was so nervous about Lloyd's well being that he was intent on sitting by the corral gate all evening. Phil reckoned that the banker wouldn't be right in the head until his horse came back—*if* his horse came back.

Word of the Indian attack had caused a commotion in town. Old women wailed about the state of the world, and young women worried about the future of their sons. Men grew uneasy, thinking that this much trouble in such a short period of time was an evil omen, and prepared to gear up for battle with Indians. As usual, Mayor Don Rombert was oblivious to the events unfolding around him. Rombert had been lying drunk on the back porch of his office all day long. Phil reckoned it was a crying shame that the townspeople didn't band together and demand that Rombert clean up his act and offer more to the community. Alas, folks in town were used to ignoring their lackluster mayor and the thought of threatening his political position before the next election had most likely never occurred to the majority of Dry Heat's residents. Besides, Larry Tulmacher was more than happy to offer public support for the townspeople. As soon as he heard about the Apache attack he had gone into one of his long, rambling, excitable speeches. It was, he proclaimed, a war between the civilized and the savage, and if the righteous were to prevail, they must band together. If he was made mayor, he promised, he would see to it that more weapons were brought into town. After all, Tulmacher had declared, smiling brightly, the more weapons a town had the less trouble they got with Indians. The sheriff wondered about that declaration—if a town was known to have an abundance of weapons, wouldn't that heighten the chances of everyday barroom brawls and neighborhood fights ending in blood? Furthermore, if the weapons were stored in a certain area, wouldn't that make the town a target of every gun-lusting bandit in the West?

Hugh Gardener had been taken to the doctor's quarters the second he got back to town. He had wailed like a newborn baby when the arrow was removed from his shoulder, but he seemed like he was recovering well when Phil saw him about an hour later. By that time Hugh was resting in bed and color was starting to creep back into his face. Billy Noonan, Dry Heat's physician, said the wound was clean and the arrow had been easy enough to dislodge. There was no sign of infection, and Dr. Noonan reckoned that the wound would heal quickly and Hugh's shoulder would be fully functional in a few weeks. The wound would leave only a scar as a reminder of his Apache encounter.

If the sheriff had been happy to hear the good news about Hugh then D.B. and Louise Gardener had been ecstatic. The Gardeners had been at their son's bedside since he had been brought to the doctor's quarters. Both the general store owner and his wife had been worried sick. When the sheriff saw them it looked as if Louise had shed every tear she had in her body and D.B. had aged fifty years. Every time Phil tried to relax he saw the worried faces of the Gardener family and his anger towards Katie washed over him again. Even as he sat attempting to relax in the saloon, Phil could not rid himself of angry thoughts.

Deputy Ron was not plagued with such bitter feelings. Grateful and amazed to have survived the last two days intact, he was happily sipping his whiskey and staring longingly at Carrie, who was scurrying around the saloon waiting tables. Ron had been watching Carrie for the better part of ten minutes when she suddenly hit a dry spot patron-wise and headed out the back door.

She's takin' her break! Ron thought happily and abruptly stood up, shaking the table and spilling some whiskey on Phil's shirt.

"Where you goin'?" the sheriff asked, wiping his shirt.

"Gotta make water, be back in a bit."

In truth, Ron had no need to relieve himself. After two straight days of putting his life on the line, the deputy wanted to have a proper talk with the barmaid in case he never had the chance again. Ron shuddered from the sudden chill as he stepped outside. The desert was a funny place; during the day it could roast your skin and at night it could freeze the blood in your veins. Carrie was standing toward the end of the building, leaning against the backboards of the saloon and staring up at the sky. Taking a deep breath, Ron managed to utter, "Howdy."

The sound of his voice made Carrie jump. She turned so quickly in surprise that a small dust cloud formed around her feet. Her face was a mixture of trepidation and defensiveness. Ron reckoned that she looked like a frightened cat in the presence of a big, mean dog.

"I'm sorry!" Ron stammered, feeling his face turning red. "I didn't mean to frighten you, ma'am."

"It's okay," Carrie replied with a little laugh, visibly attempting to gain her composure back. "I ain't used to nobody else comin' out here that's all. What are you doin' out here anyway?"

"Reckon I'm here to talk to you," Ron replied, and was instantly mortified by his directness.

"Am I in trouble with the law, sir?" Carrie asked playfully.

"No, ma'am, not yet anyway."

"Well I reckon all's well then. I'm glad to see you back in one piece. I heard about the Indian attack an' poor Hugh."

"Hugh was hit pretty bad in the shoulder but he's gonna be just fine accordin' to Dr. Noonan."

"Well I'm glad to hear it," Carrie replied before smiling somewhat devilishly at Ron. "You know, I see you in the saloon a lot."

"Hey, I'm not that heavy of a drinker," Ron retorted half playfully, half defensively.

"I didn't mean it like that!" Carrie declared, blushing with embarrassment. "I'm just sayin' that I seen you here a lot an' I never said much to you. I see you come in here for more than drinkin'. I've seen you in here playin' cards an' shootin' darts. I also noticed that you've come to a few of my shows."

"Sure did. I reckon most of the town does. Them shows are mighty entertainin' an' you got a fine voice."

"Thank you, Deputy Harris."

"It's true an' you can call me Ron if you like. Truth be told I saw you go on your break tonight an' I figured that since I'm such a fan of yours when you're actin' I might as well get to know the person too."

"That's very sweet of you."

"So, what do you do out here all by your lonesome?"

"I look at the stars. Ain't they beautiful?"

They certainly were. The desert night sky was one of the most beautiful things Ron had ever seen; it looked like a black velvet blanket coated with white diamonds.

"See those three stars in a line there?" Ron asked, pointing.

"Yeah."

"That's Orion's Belt."

"What?"

"It's a constellation, based on Greek mythology. An' you see those seven clustered together over yonder? Those are called the Seven Sisters."

"Oh, I never learned none of that stuff."

"I wouldn't know it either if my pa hadn't taught me."

"He sounds like a good dad."

"Yeah. He's sick now. After ma died he kinda went downhill." Ron stopped himself and looked down at the ground; he didn't like to talk about his father's condition.

"I'm sorry to hear that. Still, you're lucky to have had him. My pop wasn't no good in no way," Carrie replied with a cold edge to her voice.

"That's a shame. Where were you raised, anyhow?"

"All over. We never could keep up with rent or good reputation in one place for too long. My childhood wasn't exactly fun. My momma died of fever when I was little an' my daddy was a slave to the bottle. I don't reckon he liked me too much. He used to threaten to sell me to the travelin' show all the time. The funny thing is that sometimes I wished he would. Sometimes I reckoned I'd be better off runnin' away with the bearded ladies an' the tattooed men. I guess that's why I love actin' so much, just to escape from my own life for a little while, you know?"

Ron didn't know the feeling but nodded sympathetically, willing Carrie to continue her story.

"I took every odd job I could while on the road with pa. I cooked an' cleaned an' sang in front of stores. As soon as I got enough money I took the train as far as my fare would allow. That's how I wound up here."

"Well I'm glad you did, ma'am," Ron replied smiling brightly. Then, turning serious, he added, "I've seen some hard times myself. My ma died when I was little of fever just like yours. Pa went to pieces after she went an' if it wasn't for the Cobweys I don't know where I'd be. An' Phil—I mean Sheriff Palmer, although he hates folks to call him by his last name—that man treats me like the son he never had."

"You're lucky you like your job. Aside from this place havin' a stage there ain't much nice about it. An' you know what I hate most? How people judge me! Folks gossip lots in this town. Women 'round these parts know what a bunch of the saloon girls get up to an' they give me the same dirty looks! Everybody just reckons I'm as bad but I ain't. I'm a barmaid I'm an actress. I ain't no more or no less."

"Well, I reckon you're one of the most honest lookin'

women I ever did see an' it's a shame some women in this town don't have the brains in their heads to see that."

"Thank you."

"It's true, an' you've got a deputy's word about that."

There was one sweet minute when Ron and Carrie stood under the stars smiling at one another. Then the sound of raucous laughter from inside the bar disrupted the moment.

"Well I best be getting back inside," Carrie declared. "Claire gets mighty mad if I stay out here too long an' she's fearsome when her temper's up."

"I can imagine." During his career he had been called into the saloon to calm Claire down on more than one occasion. It really was amazing that she had not yet managed to murder one of her patrons. "I should be getting back as well. The sheriff probably thinks I've been eaten by a wild animal by now."

"Well, then, you better let him see you're still in one piece," Carrie replied smiling, "an' we should get to talkin' more often now that we're properly acquainted. It was a pleasure talking to you, Ron."

"The pleasure was all mine, ma'am."

"Call me Carrie."

"An' I look forward to talkin' to you more, Carrie."

Carrie and Ron walked back into the saloon together, both smiling brightly. Ron felt alive with glee as he made his way back toward the table he and Phil shared. Everything had gone well! He had actually managed to speak to Carrie without making himself seem like a simpleton! Suddenly, the world seemed like a very happy place. In the front of the bar Strings was singing some love song off-key and Claire, apparently suffering from a headache, was screaming at him to shut his mouth.

So that's what all the laughin' was about, Ron thought and smiled brighter. Off-key or not, the love song seemed perfect for the moment.

Upon approaching the table it became clear that Phil had not been as fortunate as Ron had been as far as company went. Luke Arnold and Gregory, his eight-year-old son, were beside the sheriff's table. Gregory was fidgeting and looking bored, but Luke was talking like a man possessed. Ron never much cared for Luke. He was the sort of rough-edged cowpoke whose talk got tougher and tales got taller with every sip of liquor he consumed. Now that he had taken to searching for gold in Copper's Creek his attitude had become even more arrogant. Luke was convinced that he was destined to live a life of wealth sooner or later, and he had already started living with a rich man's built-in sense of entitlement.

"I tell you, Sheriff, I seen 'em there on the edge of town, livin' up near them coal mines," Luke declared, sounding both determined and belligerent.

"For how long?" Phil replied. Ron could tell from the tone of his voice that the sheriff was unhappy about being interrupted on his relaxation time.

Luke shrugged. "About a week, I reckon, definitely a few days. They found shelter a little yonder from the mines an' they ain't been too keen on leavin' it seems. I reckon there's enough rabbits out there to last 'em a good long while if they can hunt worth anythin'."

"Then why ain't I seen or heard of 'em before now?"

"Well I'm tellin' you now, ain't I? It was Gregory here who first seen 'em; he an' a few of his friends did when they was playin' out on the range. They didn't get close to 'em or nothin' an' they didn't get no trouble from 'em, but they were black, right, son?"

Gregory nodded.

"If they been there for days then why you reckon they don't move on?" Phil asked more to himself than anyone else.

"How should I know?" Luke cried, sounding highly insulted. "I ain't no black! Maybe they wanna steal somethin'! Mr. Tulmacher is always warnin' us about them thievin' anythin' they can grab!"

"Maybe they just wanna be friends, provided they ain't a part of your wild imagination, Luke," Ron declared as he seated himself.

"I an' my boy ain't lyin'! An' if y'all gonna accuse me of doin' so in the future I won't say nothin' to you about town news! I was just tryin' to do y'all a service!" Luke gave the sheriff and the deputy a cold, hard stare before he turned and walked out of the bar, dragging Gregory behind him by the arm. From behind the bar Claire threw a glass at Strings and demanded he shut his mouth and end her headache or she would strangle him.

"What you think, Ron?" Phil asked as he watched the father and son leave.

"About what?"

"About the blacks he's claimin' are up by the mines."

"Aw, I don't know. Luke ain't exactly a reliable source.

He ain't the nicest guy, he drinks more than your average hombre an' drunks make stuff up all the time. Heck, I been livin' in this town my whole life an' I never seen no black. Why would they come now?"

"Well, that war back east is over. I hear a lot of slaves got their freedom an' are headin' out West lookin' for better lives. I've heard it's dangerous for 'em near their birthplaces, real dangerous."

"You think there's somethin' worryin' if they are really up there?"

"I don't have a problem with nobody unless they make trouble for me. Skin tone don't mean nothin' to me as far as judgin' a character goes. You know that yourself, you heard about Darcy an' all."

Ron nodded kindly as Sheriff Phil stopped talking and took a swig of whiskey. Mentioning Darcy always caused him a pang of pain.

"It's Larry I'm worried about," Phil continued. "He's turnin' the mood of this town ugly. My pa was as good a man as my Uncle Henry was a cowardly one, an' my pa always told me never to listen to hateful words. He knew how to treat folks. I remember once when I was a youngin', me and Pa were comin' home from a cattle drive an' we came across this Chinaman. I reckon the fella had come out West to work on the railroad, which was still bein' built back then. He had somehow gotten a good distance away from it, though. Maybe he'd run away from the job, I don't know. Anyway, somehow he'd gotten his leg banged up pretty bad. He didn't speak a word of English an' he was mighty nervous around us, but Pa stopped an' took a look at his leg. The leg was in pretty bad shape, broken in three places, an' it looked like the poor guy had been out in the desert for days, hungry and dehydrated. Pa gave him some rations an' water an' finally got him to come back to town with us. We took him straight to the doctor's quarters where he stayed for a week. I reckon we definitely saved his leg and probably saved his life by bringin' him back here. We was gonna have him stay around town even after he got better. We figured he'd be safe here an' could get some kinda job in a store. After a month of care he was ridin' horseback fine an' walkin' again with nothing but a minor limp. He was quiet, didn't cause no harm to nobody. The man wouldn't have been no bother to us here at all. But one mornin' we woke up an' he was just gone, high-tailed it out of town in the middle of the night on the horse we had been lettin' him use. He left Pa this piece of paper though. It was all folded up to look like a bird of some kind. I've never seen nothin' like it before or since an' I reckon it's the best gift I ever saw or heard about. I still got that thing, it reminds me of Pa an' the kind of man he was. It also makes me wonder what ever happened to that Chinaman. Anyway, the whole point is it's a shame more folks ain't raised on the kind of mindset my pa raised me on."

Phil watched Ron nod and sat back in his chair. His stomach was in knots after the stressful and tiring day. If there really were a bunch of black cowboys in town alongside Larry Tulmacher and his gang then the situation could turn bad, and more trouble was the last thing the sheriff wanted to deal with. Sighing, Phil closed his eyes and rubbed his temples. He reckoned more men like his father were just what this world needed; that would make things easier on everyone—especially tired lawmen.

As the sheriff and the deputy rested their weary bodies at Claire's Cactus, five men huddled around a small campfire which had been built a few yards away from one of the older and less frequented coal mines. The glow from the fire turned the men's brown skin bronze and the chill in the night air lit up their breath in small clouds. A few feet away from the campfire five horses were tied to a large cactus. The men sat on the ground, passing around coffee, beans, and cooked rabbit meat. Although the night was chilly, the rations of food meager, and the blankets thin and rough, the men were smiling and cracking jokes. Having lived most of their lives as slaves, they found that freedom, despite its trials and occasional misadventures, was one big reason to be happy.

"My horse cooks better than this, Pete," Samuel Armstrong, the youngest man in the group, teased. He was lean and skinny and easy to smile.

"Get 'em to cook for y'all next time, then," Pete replied. Pete Baker was a short, portly, balding man. He was older and grumpier than his comrades. He had seen so much bad in the world that it was hard for him to appreciate the good.

"When we tryin' the town for some food?" Clayton

Williams asked suddenly. Although he was the strongest man in the bunch he was usually the quietest, except when it came to creating new plans or changing old ones.

"I dunno," Pete replied. "They white. You know how they treat us."

"Back East, sure," Jonas Jackson declared, "but here's different. Ain't no room for no evil here. The Lord be's lookin' out for us at long last. He the one who give us our freedom." Jonas was a deeply religious man. Hefty and strong both mentally and physically, he embraced every issue, each problem, with a smile and strong faith. No matter how bad life got, Jonas never gave up hope.

"There's room for everythin' out here includin' ten shades of evils. We best stay put for now," Pete retorted, staring at Jonas coolly. "I don't wanna wind up on the wrong end of no rope."

"It's better out here," Jonas replied unflinchingly.

"We think so," Jack Freedman stated as he spooned his ration of beans. He was a medium-built and medium-weight man with a thick beard. Although he looked the least memorable of all the men, his quick mind and fair judgment had made him the unofficial leader of the group from the start. "The folks down there don't seem so bad, but it's better to be safe an' keep away. We already been here too long but it's the best rabbit huntin' we come by. We'll be movin' out come a few days time so there's no need to go down to them folks."

"Yo' sure you wanna go to California?" Clayton suddenly asked. "It's a big place an' it could be mighty unfriendly. I don't know nothin' 'bout cities. I been workin' the land my whole life."

"We ain't gonna be near no cities; California has out-skirts," Jack replied. "It'll be a better life than what we had before."

"An', God willin', no mo' rotten beans like Pete's been feedin' us," Samuel declared playfully, causing all the men to chuckle, even Pete. Their laughter filled the chilly night air with warmth as the moon shone down wistfully. In that moment, there was not the slightest indication of just how close to Dry Heat the five freed slaves would become in a matter of days.

Chapter Seven

The night after Phil and Ron drank their whiskey and the black cowboys ate their rabbit meat, Katie rode toward her family's new home. The moonlight was all that guided her now but the day had been bright and clear, and Katie had seen the shack on the horizon with the last light of sunset. Now she was riding hard to reach it despite the thick blanket of night. Normally, once nightfall rolled in, Katie settled down until sunrise, but when she saw the shack she knew it could belong to no other family aside from the Hubbards. It was considerably bigger than the one they had shared in Dry Heat but it had the same rambling, dirty, forlorn look about it. Katie could clearly see candlelight emanating from within the cracks in the woodwork. The Hubbards were home.

The closer she got to her family the more Katie's stomach knotted. She didn't love her family. They had never caused her anything but trouble and pain, and she had often considered herself cursed to have been born into their ranks. Her life with them was unbearable at the best of times and they had parted on bitter terms. Yet, now that Dwayne was dead, she had nowhere else to go. Besides, Dwayne's murder could not go unpunished. What was the point of coming from an infamous family unless you could use them for revenge purposes? The one thing Katie and her kin shared was their mistrust and dislike for the townspeople of Dry Heat—surely the notion of causing the townsfolk grief would arouse her family's interest.

As usual, the Hubbards were on guard looking for strangers and possible threats; before Katie was twenty yards from the house a man stepped out of the doorway shadows and pointed a rifle at her. He was young and sturdy looking, undoubtedly one of her cousins, but from the distance it was hard to tell which one. As she looked at the gun Katie felt unease so extreme that it crossed into terror—just how angry was her family toward her after all these years?

The closer she got to the house the more Katie reckoned that the man with the gun was her cousin Leroy. Leroy was strong and intimidating, but Katie was happy to see him. She was younger than him by three years and, Leroy had a soft spot for her since they were toddlers. When she was about ten feet from Leroy, Katie called out to him.

"Howdy, Leroy!" It threw the young man off guard. "Don't you remember me?"

Leroy's brow deepened, puzzled. Katie continued her approach, painfully aware of how much she was risking her life; Leroy was known to be quick to pull a trigger. Finally, after looking hard at Katie for about a minute, recognition dawned upon his face.

"Katie," he whispered lowering the gun, his eyes wide with shock and, Katie hoped, happiness. Suddenly, Leroy turned and ran into the ramshackle house screaming something that sounded like, "Katie's home, y'all!" The echoing joy of Leroy's voice was music to Katie's ears; at least one Hubbard was happy to see her. She remained mounted on Sugar, feeling as nervous as a person could get. If her family turned her away, she had no idea where she would go or what she would do. In truth, she hadn't considered the possibility of rejection until she had arrived on her estranged family's doorstep.

One by one the Hubbards emerged from within the depths of their home like hornets coming out of a hive: Siblings and half-siblings, aunts, uncles, cousins, and a number of small children whom Katie had never seen before.

"I see a few youngin's been born since I been gone," Katie remarked conversationally as she eyed the latest additions to her family. A few grunts were the only replies she received.

"Where you been, sis?" a familiar voice asked. Looking up, Katie saw Amanda, her favorite sister, standing in the doorway. Amanda was smiling her trademark crooked, somehow scheming, smile that Katie had missed so much.

Amanda looked the same as Katie remembered—skinny and tall with a shock of red hair. She was one of Katie's full sisters and the resemblance between them was undeniable. Behind Amanda stood Katie's unsmiling parents, Gilroy and Roberta Hubbard.

"I made a mistake by stayin' in Dry Heat," Katie declared, looking at Amanda. "I made a big mistake an' I paid for it. Dwayne's dead, the sheriff an' the deputy an' a few others from town killed him an' made it look like an accident. They want folks to think I'm makin' up stories, losin' my mind but I know my husband ain't dead by no accident."

"So that fella's finally gone an' left you, did he?" Gilroy sneered. He wasn't a man known for kindness or sensitivity and he had always harbored an acute dislike of Dwayne.

"Dwayne didn't leave me, Daddy! He was killed by them townsfolk like they been killin' us for years!"

"That boy wasn't one of us in no way!" Roberta hissed, outraged. Katie's mother was the one person who had hated Dwayne more than Gilroy.

"Well, he married me so that made him as good as one of us to them townies."

"Katie," Amanda said softly with an undeniable trace of tenderness to her voice, "how did Dwayne get killed?"

"They fooled his soft head into thinkin' that a cougar was out for blood up on the Sand Sun Mountains. Dwayne was always so willin' to help folks that he went on up there with a lawman's posse thinkin' that he was gonna make a big old difference in killin' the vermin. Once the sheriff an' his men had 'em out there they held him down an' got a rattler to bite his throat out."

"An' why you reckon they did that?" Gilroy sneered, obviously pleased with the brutal way in which his son-in-law had died. "That boy wasn't worth the snake's poison."

"They wanted to get back at me for stayin'!" Katie screamed, her voice cracking, her face burning, and her eyes wet. "Y'all left an' I stayed an' them townies figured that if I was gone then they'd be rid of us once an' for all! But I didn't leave so they punished me by takin' away the one thing I loved! Killin' me would have been too kind. Them townies figured that killin' Dwayne would destroy me, make me kill my sorry self. An' I almost did, I swear I almost did when I saw his body!"

"Well, you're still here now," Roberta remarked, sounding bored with her daughter's grief. "Why'd you come back here to us?"

"Help. Revenge."

"Revenge?" Gilroy exclaimed, sounding both amused and disgusted. "What that got to do with us? He was your man, not ours. Girl, you got a gun an' I taught you how to shoot, handle it yourself."

"I don't want no fast an' simple revenge like that. The sheriff would gun me down in about three seconds flat. No, I want revenge that sticks to 'em, revenge that hurts 'em years from now, revenge that leaves a gaping hole in 'em, revenge that gives 'em a taste of their own medicine. I can't do that alone. I need a group to gang up on 'em with, the same way they ganged up on Dwayne. Y'all good with guns an' y'all my kin. Don't kin help each other?"

"Why should we risk our hides on account of that fool you married who got himself killed?" Roberta asked, sounding absolutely appalled by the idea of avenging her son-in-law.

"If not for me then for your own sake, your own honor," Katie replied coolly. "Them lawmen been out to get us for years, all types of lawmen from all types of towns. Don't y'all want some justice on account of all they done to us?"

Katie stared down at her family from atop her fidgeting and exhausted horse. The Hubbards looked back at her with mixed emotions. Some looked bemused, some looked confused, and others looked wary. Amanda was the only person in the group who looked at Katie with any degree of empathy or kindness. Amanda was the one person who knew just how much Katie had loved Dwayne, and it was obvious that she understood the amount of pain her sister was in. After a number of tense, silent moments Gilroy sighed and gestured toward the house.

"I don't know how I feel about seen' you again but you're kin an' you here now," he informed his daughter before glancing at Sugar. "Besides, that horse of yours looks tired enough to lie down an' die. Put her in the corral and come inside, we got us some catchin' up to do."

If the shack was a sore sight on the outside, then the inside was diabolical. It was twice as big as the Dry

Heat house but it was three times smellier, darker, and dirtier. Despite its many spacious rooms and rambling hallways, the house was filled with stolen items and broken objects to the point that it seemed as cramped as a tomb. Of course, the house was vastly overpopulated; at least three people were in each room. Children ran around the dirt floor barefoot and half dressed. The wails of babies echoed from seemingly every room. The feeling of being an ant in an anthill reminded Katie of what life had been like growing up and the memory discomforted her. She had escaped this dirty, desperate life by marrying Dwayne and he had treated her like a queen. Now that Dwayne was dead she was back to being the same dirty, poor, miserable Hubbard girl she had been.

"I reckon you ain't got no youngin's," Roberta declared looking at Katie.

She's older, fatter, an' grayer, but she ain't mellowin' none in her old age, Katie thought before answering. "Naw, Dwayne caught sick with scarlet fever when he was a youngin' so he couldn't make no babies."

Roberta snorted laughter as if this information was the funniest thing she had ever heard. "Lord God, that man couldn't do a thing right if you gave him all the chances in the world!"

Katie was led into a dingy room in what seemed to be the center of the house. It was decorated with chairs and tables; playing cards and empty liquor bottles dotted the floor. Back in the Dry Heat house there had been a square sitting room which her father had used as a place to play cards and drink. It was also the room where important family business—like places to rob and things to steal—was discussed. Gilroy sat himself on a chair and stared at Katie. He had aged since she had last seen him—his gray hair was turning white and the lines in his face were getting deeper, yet he had managed to maintain his muscular build.

"I know you're tired an' hungry, but until you tell me exactly what you're plannin' in that head of yours, I ain't givin' you no comforts," he remarked coolly.

"I'll tell you what I'm thinkin' if you promise to help me."

"I ain't promisin' nothin' until I hear the details!"

"I need your help, Daddy!" Katie screamed with such ferocity that the walls shook. "I need y'all to come back with me an' git even an—"

"Don't you go tellin' me what I can an' can't do—"

"What in the name of stampedin' cattle is goin' on out here?" a loud, gruff voice shouted from within the depths of the house. The shout was followed by heavy footfalls.

"Who's that?" Katie asked, but before Gilroy could answer a big, burly man burst into the room. He was easily six feet tall and his long hair and beard were as black as a bat's wing. His left eye was as black as coal, and his right was covered by a patch.

"Katie, this here's Blackeye," Gilroy declared matter-of-factly.

"Where you come from?" Katie asked Blackeye. She was astounded by his presence; the Hubbards hardly ever let anyone else into their circle. Maybe he had married one of her sisters or cousins; why else would he be in the vicinity of the Hubbard family? Although Katie couldn't say that she had ever seen the man before, the name Blackeye sounded somehow familiar.

"He lives here," Roberta exclaimed before Blackeye could say a word to Katie. "He an' you should have lots to discuss. He's another one who's seen trouble in Dry Heat."

For the next half hour Katie listened to how Blackeye had met the Hubbards. The Hubbards had been gone from Dry Heat for eight months and had just finished building their new house and corral when they discovered Blackeye attempting to steal one of their horses in the dead of night. Gilroy had aimed a pistol at Blackeye and probably would have shot him to death on the spot had Roberta not come out of the house with a lantern. Gilroy knew Blackeye's face from the moment the light hit him. He had never met the man in person before the horse-stealing incident, yet he had seen his face on wanted posters in every town in the West. Blackeye was a thief and a criminal and that made the Hubbards feel right at home in his presence.

When Blackeye had crossed paths with the Hubbards, he was newly escaped from a Dry Heat jail cell. He had only the clothes on his back, a few gold coins, his guns, and his horse which he had retrieved before riding out of town. He was free but, having nowhere to go, was aimlessly wandering the desert. When he saw the Hubbard property he reckoned that they were honest farmers and it would be easy to steal a horse from them. At the time, he had reckoned that he would sell the stolen horse for enough money to get him far away from any place where he might be recognized. Of course, once he met the Hubbards everything changed. Noting that he was another outcast from Dry Heat, the Hubbards had established terms with Blackeye, which were friendly enough to constitute him living in their home. He was an accomplished criminal who knew how to plan foolproof robberies. He embraced the Hubbard style of living and he was useful to them.

A match made in heaven, Katie thought as she looked from her family to Blackeye. *They all deserve each other.* And then, with a pang of realization, *An' I guess I fit right in with 'em now.*

"So what about you?" Katie asked Blackeye, pushing the depressing thoughts to the back of her mind. "Why you get in hot water back in town?"

"That's a long story, little miss," Blackeye replied with a smirk.

"I got time."

"An' I do like to talk," Blackeye declared as he settled himself down in a chair. The feeble furniture creaked under his considerable weight. "It all started when the sheriff an' that little deputy pet of his caught me rustlin' cattle. Normally I would've been able to shoot 'em both dead an' be on my way but I had just gotten over a mighty bad fever an' my aim was off. Was the first time I ever been caught an' I reckon it would have been the last if it weren't for that dimwitted jailer . . ."

Blackeye had been enraged and humiliated upon being captured and brought back to Dry Heat. He had never imagined himself being taken alive and the fact that he had been caught by two smalltime lawmen, one who looked barely old enough to grow a beard, only added fuel to his anger. This arrest was a blemish on his criminal record and, stripped of his weapons, Blackeye had expressed his rage by cussing and kicking all the way to the jail cell. The sheriff and the deputy had ignored his threats during the journey back to town. They had tossed him into the jail like a sack of potatoes and had then gone to give a speech to the townsfolk about the latest prisoner. Blackeye had been left alone, locked in the cell, with only the young jailer for company.

Clarence Harden had never been in the presence of a real criminal before and Blackeye had captivated his complete attention. The jailer had stared at the prisoner as if he was a vulture with two beaks. Clarence had watched Blackeye intently, every so often pacing the hallway in front of the cell looking as if he would like to say something but too intimidated to utter a word. Blackeye reckoned that Clarence looked like a nervous schoolboy on his first date. Finally Clarence had approached the cell, gulped, and spoke to Blackeye for the first time.

"Since it's just you an' me in here I'm gonna ask you to empty your pockets."

"What?" Blackeye had replied, honestly surprised.

"Well, they fixin' to hang you anyway so I might as well see what gold you got. You ain't gonna need it."

Blackeye smiled slyly, finally understanding. The

shady little jailer was trying to rob him. The youngster was plenty greedy but none too bright. He had no idea who he was dealing with. Blackeye had been a thief his whole life, he had been born and raised among the urchins of society, and he was quick–minded when it came to escape plots. The jailer had the cell keys attached to his belt, and Blackeye knew he could easily slip his arm through the bars if the jailer would only come close enough. It was perfect.

"Two things," Blackeye had declared amused. "First, how do you know I got gold on me? An' two, what you reckon you'll do if I ain't willin' to let go of it?"

"I heard change rattlin' 'round in your pockets the minute you came in here. An' I reckon I could knock you out an' claim you was attackin' me if you don't do what I say. You're a dead man anyway, ain't nobody gonna care if you get a little bruised in here."

"Got me convinced," Blackeye had replied, feigning defeat. "Them lawmen took my guns an' knife but they left me some gold in my pocket."

Blackeye reached into his pocket and pulled out a handful of gold coins. Sticking his hand between the bars, he offered the money to Clarence. With his greedy eyes upon the gold, Clarence reached out without thinking. Instantly Blackeye sprang. With one hand he grabbed the young jailer and pulled him toward the cell, banging his head against the iron bars several times as hard as he could. With his other hand Blackeye grabbed the keys and pulled them so hard that Clarence's belt snapped. When Blackeye stepped out of the cell

Clarence was lying on the ground, unconscious. Blackeye reckoned that he owed the crooked little jailer his life. Thus, Blackeye decided that in Clarence's case humiliation was better than death. After tying the jailer up and stuffing him under the sheriff's desk, Blackeye retrieved his weapons and got his horse out of the corral. The townsfolk were too involved listening to the sheriff's speech to notice the prisoner making his escape.

Looking back, Blackeye was even more furious about his Dry Heat ordeal. He reckoned he should have opened fire on the entire town. A shooting spree would have been an easy way to get revenge and, noting that everyone had been standing in the same area listening to a speech, he probably could have hit a fair number of targets. Yet, at the time, he had been unnerved by capture and the notion of a narrow escape was far more appealing than the idea of revenge. Thus, without incident, Blackeye had mounted his horse and rode far, far away from Dry Heat.

"An' then I met your folks an' wound up here," Blackeye explained, ending his story.

Katie surveyed him intently. He was a quick-minded man with an air of danger and bitterness surrounding him. He had a bad history in Dry Heat and it was obvious that he was still itching for revenge. He could be a valuable ally in her revenge plot, if he could be convinced.

"So we both seen our share of trouble in Dry Heat," Katie said. "Them folks been makin' fools of us for years. Alone we couldn't do a thing about it but together I reckon we could get some real damage done. Ain't it time we taught them folks a lesson?"

"Risky business to be gettin' into," Gilroy commented. Enraged, Katie turned towards him, her eyes bright with fury.

"So what you want me to do, Daddy? Let it go? Let 'em get away with all of it? They killed my husband an' they treated my family like dirt! Don't you think they oughta pay for that? Or are you just scared of goin' after them folks? That ain't like you, not the way I remember you. As you get on in years, are you gonna be a *coward?*"

Katie hissed the last word so harshly and gave Gilroy such a cruel look that the man jumped up and approached his daughter, fists waving.

"Your little girl's got a point, Gilroy," Blackeye declared, his words stopping Gilroy from striking Katie. Blackeye's tone of voice was conversational. He was sitting back in his chair picking his teeth with a long fingernail, unperturbed by the possibility of violence. "They have done us wrong an' nobody should get away with that. A few of us could plan somethin' special for them folks, show 'em who's boss."

Gilroy considered the idea, "I suppose . . ."

"An'," Roberta added, "there's lots of places to loot in that town. We could get us years worth of supplies if we helped ourselves to the stock."

"We could get ourselves revenge an' a good livin'," Daddy," Katie commented softly.

"Allright," Gilroy replied grudgingly after a moment of silence, "let me hear your idea of a plan."

"I knew you'd come to your senses," Blackeye declared, joyfully slapping Gilroy on the back so hard that the smaller man nearly lost his balance. "I'll be lookin' mighty forward to gettin' back to that town. I got me some bones to pick an' a few skulls to crack."

Standing to the side of the room, camouflaged among her kin, Katie smiled. Her plan had worked. Vengeance would be served.

Chapter Eight

"Thank the Lord he's home an' he's safe!"

Sheriff Phil awoke with a start hearing Willis' joyful declaration. After untangling himself from the bed sheets, Phil looked out of his small, dusty, cobweb-coated bedroom window. Willis was running around on the street like an excited child and pointing at his horse. The mustard-colored pinto was bent over the water pail drinking steadily. During the night Lloyd had returned, hungry and thirsty, but alive and seemingly unharmed. Phil thought that the horse's safe return was a miracle considering the animal had been missing for two days. The sight of the horse and the banker reunited brought a smile to the sheriff's face, a rare occurrence so early in the morning. Yet his smile vanished when he eyed the dark clouds looming in the distant sky.

103

The elders were right, that dust storm is comin' in an' it's comin' in fast.

Phil lamented the past three days of bad luck and chaos as he dressed. If things continued at this rate, he would surely drop dead from a heart attack. Cynically, he wondered if he would be pushing up daisies by Saturday; perhaps Cynthia would arrive in time for his funeral. Yet death would be too easy. Life had always forced Phil to do things the hard way and this storm would be one of the hardest things to prepare for. Phil had lived through his share of dust storms and he knew how dangerous they could be. He had seen folks lose their lives on account of sand filling up their lungs. Only a few decades ago, every time there was a sand storm livestock died by the dozens; an expensive loss to many ranchers. Although Phil rarely had anything good to say about his Uncle Henry, the former sheriff of Dry Heat, he was grateful that the man had the sense to install a number of safety areas around the outskirts of town. The safety areas were large barns where livestock were protected from bad weather. Henry had installed them after the dust storm of 1841 had killed hundreds of cattle.

It was still early. Once Ron arrived for work, Phil would enlist his help to prepare everyone in Dry Heat to move into Claire's Cactus to wait out the storm. Claire's Cactus was the largest building in town and the sheriff could only hope that it was sturdy enough to withstand the winds. Of course it would need extra padding around the walls to keep sand from blowing in between the cracks in the old wood. Still, in emergency situations, it was better that everyone stay together to avoid trouble and the saloon was the only place big enough to fit the town population.

As he prepared his morning coffee, Phil thought about what needed to be done. Judging by the position of the clouds, he reckoned he had three to four hours to get Dry Heat in order. Claire's Cactus needed to be boarded up and extra blankets and food would need to be available for the people who would be waiting out the weather inside its walls. As many animals as possible needed to be put into the various safety barns, and everyone would have to be warned not to walk outside during the storm. It was a full week's worth of work in one morning.

Finishing his coffee, Phil walked outside and gazed at the black clouds moving over the horizon. His only hope was that the storm would blow its course quickly and with limited loss of life.

A half hour later the town was bustling with people preparing to withstand the oncoming bad weather. Cowpokes corralled livestock into barns as townsmen placed boards against the windows and doors of their stores and homes. Women scurried around the town collecting blankets and food to bring to the saloon. A dust storm could last a few hours or a number of days and, although the elders who had lived in town the longest thought this storm would be on the short side, it was better to overstock than understock.

By noon, the sheriff and the deputy were inside Claire's Cactus. To make the saloon more spacious chairs were being stacked on top of tables and then leaned up against the wall. It was tedious work, and the lifting wasn't exactly great for Phil's back, but it needed to be done and the more hands that helped the faster the work went.

There was a sense of urgency that prompted everyone to pitch in with the safety preparations.

Peggy Cobwey assisted the elderly in walking up the saloon's front steps as Carrie handed water to exhausted cowpokes. Dr. Noonan and Nick Stooker organized tables and chairs as Wendy Philips helped mothers control over-excited children. Even Mayor Rombert was being helpful—he was passed out behind the bar with a bottle of gin and completely out of the way of the working townspeople.

Although Phil had overheard him complaining about being tired less than a half hour before, Larry Tulmacher was doing his share to board up the saloon. He seemed uncharacteristically nervous, which made Phil wonder if Larry was one of those folks who turned yellow at the idea of a storm. Adeline Doherty was fluttering around him with a glass of water, smiling brightly and wearing way too much makeup. It was no secret that the widower was sweet on the politician. Edwina was standing in the center of the room; too vain to offer assistance, she was instead eyeballing the area in search of Ron, who had managed to camouflage himself in the busy saloon. Amelia, who was usually the most aggressive Doherty in the pursuit of Ron, had walked away from her mother and sister and, never even giving a glance around for the deputy, made her way over to Clarence, who was nailing a board against a window. The look on Clarence's face suggested that he wasn't happy about ensuring that no one would be cut by flying glass if the powerful winds were to break the window. He looked annoyed at being asked to perform such a menial task and the company of Amelia only seemed to irk him more. As usual, Amelia was in one of her much–too-revealing dresses. Although Phil couldn't hear her voice over the noise in the saloon, he could tell from reading her lips that she was flirting hard with the preacher's nephew.

Looks like Ron's got one less of 'em battleaxes to worry about, Phil thought with a chuckle as he turned his attention back to the work at hand.

The sheriff managed to stack five more chairs atop a table before the door to the saloon burst open and a group of three boys came running up to him. They were dusty, dirty, and panting as they tried to catch their breath to ease the stitches in their sides. They were around eleven years of age with extreme excitement and a touch of fear upon their faces.

"Sheriff Palmer!" the tallest boy cried, prompting the sheriff to turn from his work, annoyed.

"Phil! It's Sheriff Phil! Don't nobody call me by my last name! I've said it a million times; if Phil was good enough for my mama, then its good enough for y'all!"

"Okay, Sheriff Phil," the boy replied unfazed, "there's a shootout on the coal mines."

"What?"

"We swear!" the smallest boy in the group pro-claimed. "We heard lots of shootin' goin' on when we was behind the church. It had to have been comin' from the mines."

"How many are shootin'?"

"We don't know," the middle boy replied. "We was behind the church diggin' up a jar of marbles we hid an' as we was diggin' we heard guns bein' fired, lots of 'em. We didn't see nothin' though. I bet it's still goin' on."

"Stay indoors," the sheriff instructed the boys as he turned and studied the room looking for Ron. Noting that the Dohertys were present, the deputy was standing in the corner surveying the saloon warily.

"We've got a problem," Phil announced as he ap-proached him.

"I know, I saw 'em come in."

"Not the Dohertys! We got us a real problem, a shootout."

Ron's eyes grew wide as the sheriff told him about what the boys had said.

"I thought everyone was here!" Ron declared. "Maybe it's just a bunch of Injuns fightin' each other. That ain't none of our concern. They fight with each other all the time an' plenty of tribes been pickin' up guns in these past years."

"You could be right but ain't you noticed that Larry an' Clarence are here but the rest of Larry's men are gone? I reckon they could be upstairs but I ain't seen 'em all day, an' I got a feelin' that lot is up to no good out there. It's too much of a coincidence that they're missin' at the same time as a shootin's going on. I got a hunch we should check on this."

"This don't seem like no kind of good plan, Phil," the deputy declared, determined but still respectful. "Normally, you know, I don't mind goin' out of my way to look into some possible wrongdoin', but the horses are in the stable an' a storm's comin' in. An' not just any storm, this is a storm that will more likely than not kill any man caught out in it. We don't even know if those gunshots are our problem. This ain't safe, it's reckless. It ain't like you."

"Things ain't safe now, sure, but if somethin' is really goin' on up there that concerns this town an' we let it go, the future result could be far worse. I just got a feelin' we need to see the issue for ourselves, an' you know that I ain't never been wrong when I get a certain inklin' about trouble. If we ride over there an' it turns out that this shootin' ain't none of our concern, we'll head back straight away. We'll have time judgin' by the winds, an' I've lived through enough of these storms to know how the wind gets before they hit. We do have time. An' if we get caught out there we can wait out the storm in the mines; the way the winds blowin' shouldn't make that a problem. What you think?"

"What about the horses?"

"They're faster then us, we'll dismount an' send them back this way. The less weight they have the faster they'll run an' the easier they'll make it back to town. We'll have Willis an' some guys here waitin' for them. The storm's gonna hit the mines before it hits town so they'll be out-runnin' it."

Ron stared at Phil with conflicting emotions. He was uneasy with the plan; it seemed rash and dangerous. It was uncharacteristic of Phil to make such an important decision so quickly without thinking it out first. On the other hand, it was true that the sheriff had never been wrong about the inklings he got, especially those regarding crime. Although the deputy was unsettled by the idea of putting himself and his horse in danger, he was even more unsettled by the idea that bandits could be up on the coal mines robbing and shooting innocent folks. The coal mines were a logical place to wait out the storm for people who had nowhere else to go, and bandits took advantage of people in desperate situations. Sighing, Ron nodded at Phil.

"I'll go tell Willis an' some others what's goin' on just in case anyone asks about us."

Ten minutes later, the sheriff and the deputy rode toward the coal mines with the sound of gunshots making their ears ring. They approached the mines from behind, not wanting to surprise the shooters. Secretly, Phil was hoping that they had stumbled upon a group of warring Indians, something which they had nothing to do with and could ride away from unnoticed. Yet Phil's hope was extinguished the moment he laid eyes on the scene. Larry's cohorts and five dark-skinned men were having themselves a mean shootout. Phil saw no bodies on the ground, but it was clear from the ferocity of the fight that this one would be to the death.

A bullet suddenly flew past Ron, missing his brow by less than a foot. One of Larry's men—Phil thought he was known as Scotch—had turned his scruffy face toward the lawmen and started firing. Instinctively, the sheriff and the deputy grabbed their weapons and returned gunfire. The sudden burst of noise from the guns startled Crow and Nita, who reared up and knocked off the lawmen. The startled horses ran back toward town as Phil and Ron stood up and continued firing until one of their bullets succeeded in hitting Scotch, instantly dropping him to the ground.

Noticing who Scotch had been shooting at, two more of Larry's men had turned and took aim at the lawmen. Returning fire while ducking to avoid the bullets flying in their direction, Phil and Ron scrambled through the sand and slid behind the entranceway of an old mine.

Between the smoke from the guns and the incoming storm blowing sand in every direction, Ron was having trouble seeing what was in front of him. Although he could hear Phil firing, Ron's eyes were stinging and it was difficult to steady his hand enough to take aim and shoot. Every few seconds the wind died down, and Ron was able to see the outlines of the men shooting at him. They were undoubtably Larry's men, and there were a number of large sacks in the sand beside them. The strange sight was enough to make Ron force his eyes to focus and his mind race with questions. What were Larry's posse doing near these abandoned mines when a sandstorm was blowing in? Why did they have those sacks, and what was in them?

Ron raised his gun and fired three shots. He couldn't aim well but he hoped that the bullets would do some good. As the battle raged on and Ron reloaded his gun, he prayed; he reckoned that this could be the last chance he would ever have to do so.

Chapter Nine

Carrie had never seen Claire's Cactus so crowded; there was no direction she could look without having at least three dozen people within her view. She reckoned that the saloon looked like the inside of a beehive, busy and chaotic. Ever since she was a child Carrie hated large crowds; there was just something so intimidating—almost threatening—about a group of people large enough to constrict movement. Carrie felt like she was about to suffocate in the overwhelmingly busy saloon and the very thought of such a horrible death made her feel weak. She needed to get away from the thick crowd, and she needed to make her escape quickly. Undoubtedly, Claire would be annoyed with her for removing herself from behind the bar without permission, but three others girls were working and could easily cover for her. Besides, Carrie knew that if she was to suddenly faint—or panic—that would add even more trouble to an already hectic situation.

At the end of the bar Clarence was sitting on a stool and cradling a glass whiskey. Amelia was beside him, talking a mile a minute and leaning into him so much that she was almost resting on him. Although Clarence did nothing to encourage or divert the Doherty girl's attention, he was far from thrilled by her presence. Clarence was picky about the women he paid mind to and Amelia—although flirty—wasn't his type. Amelia was outlandish and opinionated. She wasn't hard to look at but she wasn't exactly beautiful either. Clarence's ideal woman was someone subtly beautiful, soft spoken, and undemanding. He wanted a woman who would make him appear respectable, a woman who would provide the proper image for him to become mayor after Larry was gone. After all, Tulmacher was not a young man, and Clarence had to think about the future. In short, Clarence wanted someone who wouldn't embarrass him, someone respectable looking who would be easy to control. Amelia, with her flirty clothes and demanding personality, simply did not fit the bill. The barmaid was more his type.

Clarence had been watching Carrie for a number of weeks and, the more he saw, the more he liked. He had made a number of advances toward her but she rebuked each one. Although it was obvious that Carrie didn't like him, Clarence was unwavering. He had learned to be persistent; Larry had taught him that nothing great came without a struggle, and that was a wise lesson. As Carrie walked past him, Clarence gave her arm a firm tug.

"You allright?" he asked noting her glassy eyes and pale skin.

"I'm fine," Carrie replied, attempting to pry herself away from the preacher's nephew. "I just need some restin' time."

"You can rest right here!" Clarence declared, pushing Amelia out of her chair and offering it to Carrie.

"What do you think you're doin'?" Amelia shrieked, struggling to regain her balance and outraged to be surpassed by a barmaid.

"No," Carrie declared, looking right at Clarence and ignoring Amelia, "I need a real rest, not just a sit down on some old stool."

"What makes you think she's even worth sittin' next to?" Amelia shouted at Clarence. "Ain't I been entertainin' enough? Or do you just like older women?"

Clarence turned his head to answer Amelia but Carrie didn't hear his words. The second his grip loosened on her arm she shook him away and pushed her way through the crowd in a half-run until she reached the stairway.

Once I get to my room I'll be fine, she told herself over and over again, desperately fighting the panic that was trying to wash over her. Carrie ascended the stairs quickly, grappling for her room key. The stairs and the hallway were packed with inebriated cowpokes. The upstairs corridor was the notorious area where Claire put those who had consumed too much alcohol and had nowhere else to lie. Trying not to step on any of the snoozing men at her feet, Carrie reached her door and put the key in the lock.

The comforting look of her spacious room was enough to make Carrie feel weak with relief. As she stepped into the room—her vacant heaven—thoughts of a nap filled her head. She decided that she would rest for a half hour, calm herself, and go back downstairs to help out a bit more. If she felt a panic coming on again she would return here. Carrie was so wrapped up in her thoughts that she barely registered that her door was not closing behind her. Puzzled by the absence of the securing click of the door latch, she turned and saw an aging cowpoke leaning against her door. He was staring at her hungrily. The smell of whiskey surrounded him like buzzards circling a carcass.

"You got yourself a nice, cozy, little place here, miss," he slurred.

"Thank you," Carrie replied uneasily, "but this room ain't open to the public so you best be getting out of it now."

Although Carrie tried desperately to push her door closed, the man was more persistent than she had thought, and stronger. Not taking the hint to leave, the old drunkard slid further into her room. Noting the gleam in the man's eyes, she felt a pang of real fear.

"Come on, miss, a storm's about to come through mighty strong. Can't you give a fella some company?"

"Get out now!"

"You're a feisty one," the man replied, chuckling.

He had walked a good five feet into the room, leaving the door standing wide open. All the exhaustion that Carrie had felt just moments before had morphed into stone-cold fear. She needed to get out of the room and away from this man, and she needed to make her escape quickly. Gathering up all her courage, Carrie sprinted toward the door. She knocked the old drunk against the wall as she passed, causing him to fall against the wood so hard that the room shook. Carrie was barely three feet down the hall when the drunk was behind her again. He was cussing wildly as he pursued her with vengeance and he was much faster than she would have thought possible. It was hard to move down the crowded corridor without tripping over the sleeping cowpokes that lay over almost every foot of the floor. Never before did Carrie imagine herself running toward a crowd but she reckoned that she would be safe downstairs, and surely someone would step in to help her.

Carrie made it to the top landing of the stairs before the man grabbed her. Allowing a scream to escape her lips, Carrie turned and began to hit the drunk while begging him to leave her alone. The scuffle was dizzying. Carrie was aware of her feet moving in circles and her hands beating her captor, yet she had no idea how close to the stairs she was until the man tripped. One second she was pulling his beard and screaming for him to release her and the next second he was falling backwards, one arm extended outward trying to maintain his balance, and the other holding onto her tightly.

He was falling and he was going to take her with him. Reacting instantly, Carrie grabbed the stairway railing and, holding on for dear life, kicked the drunk as hard as she could with her right leg. He let out a gasp as he lost his grip on her shoulder and plummeted down the steep stairs. Carrie watched, horrified, as his body turned over again and again until he hit the bottom landing and lay still, his neck in an unnatural position.

Despite the crowd and the noise level in the saloon, a number of patrons heard the scuffle and turned around just in time to watch the man's body tumble down the stairs. The second it hit the ground with a sickening thud, an old woman screamed and pointed at the body, thus drawing everyone's attention to the scene. Time stopped for Carrie as every set of eyes in the saloon stared at her.

Clarence had watched the scene unfold from where he sat. In truth, Carrie had acted in self defense, yet, given the mood of the saloon, Clarence reckoned that the truth could easily be distorted. Carrie was in an awkward position, and Clarence reckoned that after all the times she had turned him down he could finally make himself her hero. With a few right words, and maybe a threat or two, the barmaid could be his woman.

"He's dead!" Adeline Doherty shrieked as she covered Edwina's eyes. "Of all the wicked sights to cross my innocent girl's eyes, a man killed! Lord have mercy!"

"I'm sorry! I didn't mean to!" Carrie wailed from atop the stairs. She was obviously dismayed and a number of women, led by Peggy Cobwey, were moving toward her full of kind words and comfort.

"You claim what you done was an accident but it sure don't look that way to me," Clarence declared, rising to his feet and walking toward the dead man. As expected, the sound of his voice stopped the women from walking toward Carrie. Everyone remained in place, darting their eyes from Clarence to Carrie.

"What are you sayin'?" Carrie shrieked. "You don't think I wanted to kill him, do you?"

"Is Dr. Noonan here?" Clarence asked as he reached the fallen man and felt for a pulse. From across the room Dr. Noonan was already making his way toward the body. The doctor placed his hands on the old cowpoke's neck and wrist, he felt for breath under the nose before looking at Clarence and shaking his head. "Man's dead as can be. Ain't no trace of life nowhere. He was probably dead mid-fall."

"So we do got us a murder here," Clarence proclaimed.

"No!" Carrie screamed, her eyes bulging with terror. "I ain't murdered nobody!"

"It could have been an accident," Dr. Noonan replied, looking at Clarence. "He fell down, he wasn't shot."

"Well, I don't know, it seems mighty suspicious to me. The woman standin' on top of them stairs is a lot younger than the man lyin' dead at the bottom of them. I saw her up there hittin' him an' swattin' him an' he wasn't doin' nothin' to her."

"He grabbed me!"

"In attempt to balance himself and spare his life!" Clarence replied dramatically. After spending such a great deal of time with Larry, he discovered that he was developing a talent for giving dramatic speeches and getting public favor turned his way. "This man wanted to live, he didn't want to end his life here. He tried to save himself, he tried to reach out for help, an' this woman kicked him away! This was nothin' more than a cold-blooded killin'! She probably reckoned she'd get away with it notin' how busy this saloon is at the moment. She thought she could take advantage of a deadly storm an' a bunch of nervous an' distracted folks so she could end this man's life in a senseless killin'!"

"That ain't true!" Carrie shouted, her eyes bright with fear.

"It's the way I saw it," Clarence replied calmly.

"Me too!" Amelia shrieked suddenly, causing a number of startled onlookers to jump. Hearing her voice those words, Clarence felt a pang of true fondness for the Doherty girl.

"She pushed that man on purpose an' I saw it all!" Amelia continued, enjoying herself immensely. "She's nothin' but a lowdown killer an' we oughta fix her a good shot of justice. I say we hogtie her, smear her with honey, an' leave her on top of an anthill!"

"Hangin' her be much easier," Clarence replied matter-of-factly as Carrie tightened her grip on the stairway railing so she wouldn't faint.

"Now that just seems a bit harsh," Preacher Warren Harden declared from the left side of the room. "The Lord forgives an' he don't like it when we don't follow his example."

"An' he don't like killers either; you should know

that more than anyone else, Uncle. Wouldn't you say we're doin' the right thing by gettin' rid of the guilty to protect the innocent?" Clarence retorted savagely.

Warren looked like he wanted to say more but his nephew's gaze was cold and mean, and it was clear that the majority of the town was on his side. Not wanting to publicly undermine his nephew, or anger the people he was roped in with, Warren sat down feeling as weak as a one-hundred-year-old man.

"You ain't the law!" Peggy Cobwey declared from across the room. "You ain't even a politician, you're just an assistant to a possible future mayor. You can't hang nobody, only lawmen can pass such sentences. Where's Sheriff Phil an' Deputy Harris?"

"They're out investigatin' some shootin', probably Injuns with guns."

"What?" Peggy shouted, a knot instantly in her stomach. She had thought Ron was in the saloon, lost among the crowd. How could he have gone outside with a dust storm coming in? It was downright stupid! He was out playing with death and now, even if he came home alive, he would find the woman he loved either hanged or about to be hanged.

"It's true," Clarence explained. "I overheard Deputy Harris tellin' Willis the banker that he an' the sheriff were goin' up near the mines to check out some shootin' they was hearin'. That means that until they come back, *if* they come back, Mr. Tulmacher an' I are the law."

"That ain't true," Peggy replied, struggling to keep her voice from trembling. "The mayor is the law until they get back." Despite the seriousness of the situation, Peggy's remark caused more than a few snickers to spread throughout the crowd.

"Lord knows Rombert can't make no decisions, the man's unconscious with drink!" Clarence proclaimed. "An' by this time next month, after elections, it's safe to say that Larry will be the new mayor. An' since Larry's feelin' ill an' gone up to bed early, I'm in charge of the law for now. There's a good chance the current lawmen ain't gonna be comin' home; mighty fool thing to be goin' out in a storm like this. The elders reckon this storm will be over by early mornin' an' if the lawmen ain't back here by noon the prisoner is mine to hang. Now, some of y'all go up there an' get her before she decides to throw somebody else down them stairs!"

Carrie was too shellshocked to defend herself as a group of large cowpokes grabbed her, led her downstairs, and locked her inside a large storeroom. Alone in the dark, Carrie sat stock still. Her mind was numb with fear and disbelief. How could her wish to take a short nap have ended so horribly wrong? Worst of all, Ron was outside in the middle of a shootout and a sandstorm and if he didn't return by noon the next day all that would remain of Carrie Halod was a cold corpse.

Chapter Ten

The bullets had stopped coming from the other side. Beyond the blowing sand and clearing gunsmoke five bodies lay motionless.

"It over or they just playin' possum?" Clayton asked, peering over the top of his gun.

"Hard to say," Phil replied. As sheriff he was required to be the first man to inspect such a scene, but he wanted to wait a few moments to let the air clear. His right arm—his shooting arm—had been deeply grazed by a bullet during the fight and was bleeding at a steady pace. Phil used his left hand and his teeth to tie a handkerchief around his aching arm; he hoped that would ease the pain and allow him to focus.

Ron glanced over at the bleeding sheriff. Scouting a scene which could be deadly was no job for a wounded man. Holding his weapon securely and keeping one eye on the still bodies, Ron turned and faced the black men. He didn't know them, but they had helped saved his and Phil's lives so he reckoned they were trustworthy.

"We gotta make sure they ain't fakin'," Ron declared. "I'll start walkin' over there, an' if y'all see one of 'em movin', then y'all shoot."

"I'll go with you, mister." Jack replied. "This ain't no job for nobody alone."

"You sure?" Ron asked, staring at Jack with deep gratitude.

"Sure I sure. Five dead bodies ain't nothin' compared to where I come from."

Ron nodded and turned back towards the other men. "Y'all get ready now. I know you can aim well, an' if you see any movement from them bodies, don't be shy about pullin' the trigger."

As Ron crept toward the bodies, he glanced nervously at the sky. The stormy black clouds were moving fast and the wind was picking up fiercely. With every tentative step he took, sand blew into his face, making his skin feel like it was on fire. Jack reached the first body which was lying facedown. Aiming his LeMat revolver, Jack kicked the body. The man did not stir. Exercizing great caution, Jack turned the body over. The cowpoke was as dead as could be, with a bullet lodged squarely between his open eyes. From where he stood Jack could clearly see that two other men were dead. One was lying on his side with a hole in his chest and the other was lying on his back with a lake-sized pool of blood around his head. Ron was checking the other two and from the calm expression on the deputy's face Jack assumed that the shooters were no longer dangerous.

"I can't believe we got 'em all that easy, seven to five or not," Ron proclaimed as he stood up and walked toward Jack. "I was sure I was goin' to meet my maker this time."

"I guess God likes you," Jack replied as he waved to the other men, signaling that all was well. Still favoring his wounded arm, Phil walked passed Ron—the bodies didn't interest him but the sacks next to them did.

"Help me with this," Phil asked, fiddling with the strings that closed one of the sacks. The contents that spilled forth resembled something out of a king's palace: silver coins and a few pieces of jewelry followed by gold nuggets and paper dollars—lots of paper dollars.

"Lord God an' his son Jesus! Look at all that gold!" Samuel declared with wide eyes. "I ain't never seen so many riches in my life!"

"How'd it get out here?" Clayton asked.

"We didn't steal nothin' from you!" Pete declared suddenly, staring distrustfully at Phil and Ron.

"Why'd you think we'd accuse you of a thing like that?" Phil asked. "We know it ain't you that stole this gold, them dead fellas lyin' on the ground did. I reckon they were takin' orders from their lowdown leader who's back in town."

"Pete can be little nervous 'round white folks," Jack explained. "Where we come from they ain't as nice as y'all."

"I'd believe that," Phil replied, staring at the gold and

thinking about Larry. So this is why the politician had been so antsy before; he wasn't worried about the storm, he was worried about the gold and money he had stolen from the town bank. Phil reckoned that everything he was looking at was from the town vault. *The townsfolk ain't gonna like this one bit,* he thought, wondering how many weeks' worth of wages were in the three sacks.

"How'd the shootin' start?" Phil asked Jack.

"Them fellas," Jack replied pointing at the dead men. "We was plannin' on waitin' out the storm up here an' came across them carrying the sacks out of the cave. They started shootin' the minute they laid eyes on us. If we hadn't shot back they woulda killed us like they did them Injuns."

"What Injuns?"

"Couple of days ago we saw a group of white men shoot three Injuns dead right 'round here. They just took to shootin' for no reason. We didn't do nothin' 'bout it, we didn't want no problem. Anyway, I'd say these dead men are the same ones who did that shootin'."

So yesterday was an Injun revenge attack, Phil thought. *They figured we was the same men who shot an' killed some of their tribe.* Considering the reason for the attack, it was a miracle that the Indians had decided not to raid and set fire to the town. Perhaps Phil's luck really wasn't as bad as he often thought it was. Suddenly, a wind blew up with such force that it sent dust flying into the air.

"We gotta get cover," Ron cried, unable to hide the unease in his voice.

"What about the horses?" Clayton asked. Ten horses

in all—the black men's and Larry's cohorts—were still tied to cactus on opposite sides of the mine. They were naying and fidgeting, obviously frightened by the high winds and changing air pressure.

"We need to let 'em go," Phil replied. "Untie 'em, point 'em towards town, smack 'em on the hide to make 'em run, an' pray they make it to town an' someone is able to bring 'em into cover before the winds start up at full force."

"It's too risky!" Ron protested. "Let's ride back in on 'em. It's better than stayin' up here."

"There ain't time!" Phil shouted. "Look at the way this storm's blowin' up. Them horses only got half a chance at makin' it back anyway, an' they can move faster without our weight on 'em. We got a much better chance hidin' in the mines an' horses can't git into mines. It's better for us an' them to let 'em go alone. Now help me untie 'em while there's still time!"

Battling high winds and blowing sand, the men untied the ten horses and headed them toward the town. The horses took off with stampede-like speed. Satisfied that the horses had been given a fair chance at life, the men made their way into a dark mine. They dragged the sacks behind them for safekeeping; if the sacks were covered by a sand drift, it was possible they would never be found. The abandoned mine was a dodgy shelter, yet it was situated at an angle that protected the men from the wind and dagger-like grains of sand.

"I hope the horses get back okay," Samuel said after a few minutes of silence. "I always liked those animals."

"We did all we could," Phil replied. "I'll tell you, in the last few days I've done enough worryin' about horses to last me a lifetime."

"Did that yella one get back to y'all all right?" Jonas asked.

"What?" Phil replied, startled.

"We found this little yella horse yesterday. He was on his own, looked mighty scared. He wasn't easy to catch, we got a hold of him 'round sunset an' gave him some food an' water. He was breathin' real hard so we gave him a night to rest. We figured he was from yo' town since he was well looked after; he wasn't no wild beast. We didn't want to get accused of stealin' no horse by keepin' him 'round too long so first thing this mornin' we got him to run back to y'all. I was just wonderin' if he made it okay."

"He's fine," Phil replied, suddenly very fond of these new acquaintances. "His name's Lloyd an' he got separated from his owner on Monday night. We was tryin' to catch him on Tuesday when there was an Injun attack an' he got scared off again. He's the banker's horse, and the man is crazy about that animal. He was a nervous wreck thinkin' about its fate while it was gone. I know he'll want to thank you for what you done; it was mighty nice of y'all to care for him like that."

"Ain't nothin'."

"I'm Phil Palmer by the way, sheriff of Dry Heat."

Phil extended his hand to Jonas. The surprise Jonas felt upon seeing Phil's outstretched palm was indescribable. Never before had a white man offered to shake his hand. At first Jonas hesitated, yet after a few seconds he smiled and gave the sheriff's hand a hearty shake. Greetings and handshakes went around the dark mine and for a few minutes the cool cave was warm with human companionship. Then the wind shifted and streamed down the mine shaft. It echoed off the walls, wailing like a woman in bad childbirth, while cruelly blowing sand down the earthy corridor. Instantly the area which had been a safe haven became a death trap. Taken by surprise, the seven men turned toward the wall and covered their eyes with their hands. Phil suppressed a scream as high-speed wind whipped against his wounded arm and filled his right ear with sand.

"She's turned!" Ron screamed over the howling wind, "what are we supposed to do now?"

Phil had no answer. Frankly, he had no idea what they were going to do. He felt panic coming on; this was no way to die, but he couldn't think of any possible escape.

A clear, high-pitched whistle pierced the air, rising above the shrieking wind like a soaring bird. Phil turned toward the sound of the whistle with great effort. It was coming from the front of the mine in the same direction as the wind. Squinting his eyes, suffering greatly for the slightest bit of sight, he saw the shadowed outline of a young man standing in the doorway of the mine. He was beckoning the men with his hands. It was almost impossible to hear over the wind but Phil thought the figure was shouting: "Over here, follow me!"

Growing up, Phil had heard his share of ghost stories. He'd heard tales of the dead, angels, or God himself, appearing to bring the living into the next life. He wondered if the shadowed figure was something of this sort. Perhaps he had died in the gunfight and now he was being called back to wherever it was he came from. The present state of the mine was so uncomfortable that leaving it under any circumstances seemed like the logical thing to do. Although, suppose he really was looking at the angel of death, he couldn't go with him. If he did, what would become of his niece, Cynthia?

Yet this didn't seem like death. The wind was still loud enough to drive him deaf; the mine still smelled like damp earth, the flying sand was still burning his skin, and his wounded arm was still painfully pulsating. No, this scenario had none of the comforts of death, this was life. Whoever the shadowed figure was, he was of this world.

The other men had noticed the figure as well, thus relieving the sheriff that he wasn't hallucinating. Jonas was the first man out of the mine. He stumbled against the wind, struggling to keep his footing and reciting a prayer. Pete was behind Jonas, and before he knew it, Phil was running behind them. He glanced back to see the remaining men tagging along behind him. Once out in the stormy desert, the seven saved men followed the mysterious young man like ducks in a row.

Chapter Eleven

The terrain was rough and ragged and the storm was growing stronger. The wind was blowing like a whistle, making Phil's ears ring, and the sand was slapping his face like a scorned lover. The temperature had dropped to almost freezing since the thick clouds had blocked out any trace of the sun. Phil could only see what was directly in front of him—Pete's back. He hoped that Pete was still following Jonas and Jonas was still following the figure. Phil prayed that the mysterious man knew where he was going; he didn't like the idea of dying while aimlessly wandering the desert. As to where they were headed—assuming they were headed anywhere in particular—Phil couldn't even begin to guess.

Walking was an almost unbearable chore. Between the fierce wind and rapidly piling sand drifts, the sheriff felt increasingly uneasy. Yet, each time he raised his eyes and looked ahead he saw a shape forming—a large, looming, mass of a structure which rose from the ground. The closer they got, the more the structure resembled a house. Phil's suspicions were confirmed when he was led past a wooden gate into the front of a yard, up a step and through a doorway into a warm, sandless world. He was instantly enthralled by the smell of the house. It was a thick, sweet aroma which could wrap a man within it. It was a comforting, relaxing scent which reminded him of his mother's cooking.

As soon as he was sure that everyone had made it into the shelter, Phil was free to observe his surroundings. He was in a wooden house, the nicest one he'd ever seen. There were no cracks or signs of weathering in the wood. Colorful rugs, woven in intricate patterns, dotted the floor. The furniture was European-looking and, although it was well used, it was not broken or dirty. Oil lamps sat on small tables filling the room with a warm glow while the air mingled with the sweet smell of home cooking.

For the first time Phil was able to clearly see his rescuer. The shadowy figure who he had thought was the angel of death was actually a boy in his late teens with distinctive Indian features: smooth black hair and coal-black eyes with deeply tanned skin. He was staring at the men silently and inquisitively. Phil's comrades were still disoriented from the surreal experience of being brought from the center of a brutal storm into the warmth of a well-furnished home. They were staring at their surroundings so intently that they didn't even notice the young Indian before them. Everyone jumped when a door further inside the house squeaked open and a tall, raven-haired woman entered the room.

Phil recognized Mad Maggie on sight. Although Caucasian, Maggie wore traditional Indian clothing: a tan hide leather dress with beads and turquoise/silver jewelry. It was a far cry from the tattered Western attire she wore whenever she came into town. Maggie stared at the men with interest. She didn't seem alarmed by the presence of the five black men, nor did she seem irked by the extra company. Her cool blue eyes were the portrait of calmness.

"Y'all want to tell me what you were doin' up by the coal mines in this storm?" she asked with a bemused look on her face.

"It's a long story, ma'am," Phil replied, beginning to relax. The burning sensation the sand had caused his skin was just starting to dull. It was lucky they had gotten out of the storm when they did since it sounded as if it had reached full force; the winds had grown so strong that the whole house was shaking and creaking.

"We got time, Sheriff, ain't nobody goin' out in that storm," Maggie replied. "I must say, it's funny to be seein' you again. The last time I saw you was in town a few months back. Mayor Rombert was dumb drunk again an' he'd fallen in the horses drinkin' trough. You were tryin' to get him out before he drowned himself."

Hearing this statement, Samuel burst into laughter and the other men chuckled. Phil managed to crack a smile; he missed the days when intoxicated politicians were the worst of his worries. Maggie allowed the men to sit and relax. After introductions were made, Phil spent over an hour explaining how and why they had ended up trapped in a mine during a vicious storm.

"If this young fella here hadn't come our way I reckon we was goners," Phil stated as he finished his story and leaned back in his chair twitching his feet, itching to get his heavy boots off.

"Sounds like you made seven new friends today, Hawk," Maggie said to the boy standing next to her. "An' to think, I was plannin' on yellin' at you for stayin' out so long when a storm was blowing in." Smiling, she turned her gaze on Phil. "I sent him out to get cactus' prickly pear for my soup an' he disappeared on me. I was mighty worried."

"An' I got it," Hawk replied, gingerly pulling the fruit from a leather pouch at his side. "It was when I was cut-tin' the cactus that I heard the shootin' an' wanted to see what was going on. By the time I got there, I saw these men goin' into the mine an' I knew that the wind was gonna shift an' they'd be in trouble. I knew this fella was the sheriff an' so I had to do somethin'."

"How'd you know I was the sheriff?" Phil asked. He had never seen Hawk before in his life.

"I tell him all about the town," Maggie explained. "I describe everythin' in detail for him since he's never been there himself. His mother don't think he'd be safe there with his looks an' I get the same feelin' too sometimes, es-pecially from that *thing* you're lookin' to make the new mayor. Now, y'all have had a rough day so you might as well take some time to relax. Make yourselves comfortable. Hawk, go get your momma and the others an' ask them to come help me prepare some extra food."

Hawk nodded and disappeared into the depths of the house.

"This is mighty nice of you," Ron declared gratefully.

"Well, what do you expect?" Maggie replied good-naturedly. "It wouldn't be no type of goodness if I didn't fix my guests something to eat, especially when they got lawmen among 'em!"

Three women emerged from within the back rooms. Like Hawk, the women were tall with long black hair, dark eyes, tan skin, and sharp features. They passed the men hurriedly, casting them sheepish and slightly distrusting glances before disappearing into the adjoining room with Maggie. Phil was the first man to kick off his boots and rub his aching feet. He was getting too old to run around the desert. Hawk remained in the corner, staring at the men silently.

"I ain't never met a fella named Hawk before," the sheriff declared conversationally.

"Hawk's a nickname because I have good vision," the young man replied, emerging from the corner and smiling, pleased to be acknowledged. "My real name's Benjamin Murray; I'm named after my dad."

"Makes sense," Phil replied. He was just starting to get the circulation back in his toes.

"Hawk's what most people call me though," the boy continued enjoying the conversation. "I really can see like a Hawk. Maggie says my eyes are like magic because I can see stuff clearly from so far away. Its how I spotted y'all. Well, the shootin' an' my eyes together."

"Then thank the Lord for yo' eyes," Jonas declared. "That mine wasn't no place to wait out this storm."

A little less than an hour later the men were called in to the kitchen to eat. There were so many people present that chairs from other parts of the house had to be carried into the kitchen to accommodate everyone. The meal prepared was a feast fit for kings. Buttered bread, beans, flavored rice, vegetables, roasted chicken, cactus soup, whiskey, coffee, and water filled the men's stomachs to capacity. The men wolfed down the food quickly, too hungry to engage in small talk. It was not until the food was gone and the men's hunger subsided that civil conversation arose once again.

"That's some mighty fine cookin'," Clayton declared before he devoured his last spoonful of rice.

"Thank you," Maggie replied, motioning toward the three Indian women seated at the table. "But they're the real cooks. These women here are Doli, Luyu, and Angeni—Hawk's mother."

The women smiled and nodded but kept their eyes lowered and heads bent over their plates.

"I don't mean to pry, but how did you get to livin' with three Injun women?" Ron asked.

Maggie smiled. "I was wonderin' when that question was gonna come up. Y'all are the first townsfolk to know that I ain't livin' all by my lonesome."

Maggie explained that the three Navajo women had all been banished from their tribes for different reasons.

Luyu, the youngest girl, was banished because of a mental disability. Her tendency to get confused and make mistakes eventually enraged her clan who believed she was cursed and incurable. They abandoned her in the desert, assuming she would die. Maggie found her a short time after and was unable to leave the girl alone. Needing the company and noting how sweet Luyu was, Maggie took her under her wing and became a surrogate mother to the girl.

Maggie met Angeni and Hawk a few years later. Hawk was four months old when Maggie first laid eyes on him. His daddy was an Irishman whom Angeni had ran off with and married against the wishes of her tribe. A few months after his son's birth, Benjamin Murray Senior died of cholera leaving Angeni with no place to go. With her husband dead, Angeni had not felt safe in any town—most cowpokes weren't very hospitable to the women they called squaws. Going back to the tribe she had scorned was out of the question, so Angeni and Hawk had ended up living out in the desert. Angeni was a resourceful woman and she knew how to live off the land. She stayed out on the range with Hawk for a few weeks before Maggie came across them. At first Angeni didn't trust Maggie, even after the white woman offered her food. Yet, once Angeni caught sight of Luyu and spoke a few words to her in her native tongue, she quickly warmed up to Maggie. She and Hawk had been living with her ever since.

Doli was the last woman Maggie had taken in. She arrived less than two years before when she, in desperate hunger, came knocking on Maggie's door begging for something to eat. Doli was the daughter of an adviser to the tribal chief. An exceptionally beautiful girl, Doli had been promised to the tribe's most valued warrior yet the man had scared her. He was violent and brutal, and Doli had risked everything to escape becoming his bride. Although she was wise enough to take a horse and some supplies and leave in the dead of night, Doli didn't last long alone in the desert. She had been a privileged member of her tribe where others did things for her. Unlike Angeni, Doli wasn't good at hunting or cooking or finding cover from a storm. After three days by herself she was mad with hunger and, despite the risk, had knocked on the first door she saw desperately seeking aid. Maggie never forgot the look on Doli's face when she saw three more of her kind inside the house.

"She stayed here too, obviously," Maggie concluded. "I always got room for one more an' she didn't have no place else to go."

"Can they speak any English?" Ron asked.

"Not much, except Hawk who speaks both English an' his native tongue perfectly. The women speak a little English, same as I speak a little bit of their language but we don't always need words to communicate. Hawk does most of that for us anyway."

"An' you're okay out here on your own?"

"Sure we are!" Maggie replied, laughing. "I've been out here on my own longer than you've been in this world, Deputy. I manage just fine even if I do have to wear them old European clothes every time I go into town. No wonder people think I'm mad, wearin' those old rags but, as you can see, I spend most of my time wearin' clothes the girls make."

"Well, your way of livin' is a mighty kind one," Phil said. "How do you keep up with it?"

"You mean how do I survive out here without goin' to work?" Maggie asked, a chuckle in her voice. "Don't worry, Sheriff, ain't nothin' illegal goin' on out here."

For the next half hour Maggie told the men about herself. She had grown up in Texas as the only child of wealthy, kindly, late-in-life parents. Her father had been a master architect who was responsible for building half the houses and stores in their Texas town. Maggie had tended to her parents through their old age and when they died she laid them to rest side by side in the church cemetery. With her parents gone Maggie was close to no one in her birth town. Wrecked with grief, she had gathered all of her belongings in a wagon and headed west. She was looking for a quiet place to live, some place where she wouldn't be bothered by people. She chose her spot carefully. She liked the area on the other side of the coal mines because it was secluded, yet still close enough to a town so she would not be isolated in case of an emergency. She built her own house, remembering her father's lessons about creating sturdy structures, and decorated it with the furniture she had brought from Texas.

"I have a good sum of inheritance money, so when I go into town I buy everything with honest currency."

"Well, it's a relief to know I ain't got to arrest you,"

Phil replied. He had never imagined that the woman the townsfolk called Mad Maggie could be so talkative.

"You know," she continued solemnly, "when I first came out this way I was lookin' to live a lonely, quiet life. I was only a young woman; it was a crazy way to think. Back then I never would have believed that I'd be sharin' my home with three Navajo women an' a boy but they're my family now, what can I say? Life is strange."

"Ain't y'all bothered by what the folks in town might say 'bout a woman such as yo'self livin' with women like them?" Pete asked, speaking for the first time. Maggie fixed the ex-slave with a determined yet sympathic gaze.

"No, I don't," she replied firmly but kindly. "Things here ain't like where I assume you come from, not as bad anyway. I don't fear nobody in this town, I ain't got a reason to. An' I don't care what kind of crazy rules folks make up, people are people no matter what differences they got."

Phil felt his mouth curling into a smile. Maggie had the same thoughts about people he did; that was a rare occurrence, especially since Larry came to town. As Maggie stood up to collect the dinner plates she glanced over at the smiling sheriff and noticed the bloody hand-kerchief around his wounded arm for the first time.

"You're injured!" she said, pointing at his arm.

"I got grazed by a bullet up near the mines. I didn't want to trouble you more ma'am an' the bleedin's slowin' down."

"That don't matter! It could get infected. I know how to dress a wound an' I got just the right ointment to put on it. You just stay put. As soon as this table's cleared off I'll patch you up. Why didn't none of you say nothin' to me about him bein' hurt?"

"Truthfully, ma'am," Ron replied sheepishly, "between the shock of gettin' out of that storm, meetin' you, an' that dinner, I clear forgot."

The other men nodded; they, too, had forgotten.

"Ain't it nice to know that I got such a carin' posse lookin' out for me?" Phil declared, rolling his eyes sarcastically.

Once the table was clear of dishes and the other men rested comfortably in the livingroom, Maggie sat down beside Phil. He had taken off his coat and shirt and removed the handkerchief revealing the nasty wound. It was a deeper cut than he had originally thought. Maggie was right; it was the type of injury that could get infected quickly. The sheriff eyed Maggie's first aid kit suspiciously; he had never been fond of anything medical.

"Don't worry, I ain't gonna hurt you," Maggie declared as she doused a clean rag with alcohol. Yet the sheriff's suspicions were justified. When Maggie used the rag to clean his wound, the stinging pain made him jump.

"That ain't my idea of painless!" he snapped.

"Well, it'd be worse if you got an infection! You'd feel real pain then, maybe lose the whole arm. Besides, you're a sheriff, ain't you supposed to be a tough guy?"

"I'm too old to be tough."

"You don't seem that old to me."

"Well, I feel it these past few days."

Silence ruled the room for a number of minutes as Maggie tended to Phil's injury. She had placed a needle and thread on the table alongside grounded herbs he didn't recognize—most likely some sort of Indian painkiller. Phil knew that she had to stitch his arm but the thought made him queasy.

"Why did you change your mind about people all of a sudden?" Phil asked, wanting to break the silence and take his mind off his pain.

"Love," Maggie replied unflinchingly. Noticing the look of surprise on Phil's face she smiled. "I haven't had guests in a long time an' I ain't gonna be shy about answerin' any question they ask me. Anyway, about a year after I moved here I was havin' trouble gettin' this injured horse I found to water. His left foot was lame an' although he let me get close enough to put a rope around his neck, he wasn't gonna let me lead him to the creek without a fight. So there I was tryin' to pull this horse an' yellin' like the devil in frustration when I see this man on horseback comin' along in the distance. At first I was wary—a woman out in the desert all by her lonesome an' all—little did I know what was comin' my way. His name was Charles Everett, an' he was good with horses. He was able to lead that horse to water an' bandage his leg. Then we got to talkin'. He was workin' on a ranch at the edge of town which was pretty close to my place. We got along from the start an' we had a full year of seein' each other every day. I was sure we was gonna get married an' have us a life together but then he got trampled to death by a horse. After he was gone I got real depressed; I don't think I'd ever felt so alone in my life. When I found Luyu I felt like God had taken mercy on me. I helped her but she also helped me, she took away that loneliness, you know? I think the best thing Charles did for me was rekindle the need for human company, which I lost after my folks died. I know that Charlie would be happy to know that I been helpin' people these past years. That's what he always did, helped people."

Maggie stopped talking and concentrated on bandaging the sheriff's arm. Phil had heard a slight hitch and tremble in her voice towards the end of her story. It must have been a difficult subject for her to discuss since this was the first time she had gotten quiet. Before he knew he was planning to, Phil spoke: "I was in love once too, a long time ago. Her name was Darcy Mendez. She was a good woman an' we had us some good times. She drowned in a flash flood."

"I'm sorry to hear that," Maggie replied with sympathy.

"I'm sorry about Charles."

"The good ones go young, that's for sure," she declared as she finished bandaging Phil's arm, gathered her medical tools, and stood up. "Well, Sheriff, you seem to be all back in order."

"Call me Phil," he replied smiling.

"Well then, Phil, I reckon you best get some rest. I'll go put some blankets down on the sittin' room floor for y'all. I ain't lettin' none of you leave until that storm's over. An' don't put that old shirt on. Give it to me an'

I'll wash it for you. I'll get you a clean one to wear to-night. It'll be one of Hawk's an' tight on you but a tight shirt's better than a bloody one."

Phil smiled gratefully as he watched Maggie leave the room. *Findin' her was a gift from God,* he thought happily, suddenly realizing that the work Maggie had done on his arm had greatly eased his pain.

Chapter Twelve

That night, as the other men snored and the storm blew its course, Phil lay on the blanket-covered floor of Maggie's home and thought about Darcy. It was a painful subject, one he tried never to think of, but tonight her memory was fresh in his mind, yearning for attention. Although it had been twenty-seven long years since he met Darcy, it sometimes seemed as if he had been with her mere hours ago. She was always in his mind—her voice, her expressions, the way she moved—everything about her was stored away in his memory, never to be forgotten. He often heard her voice in his head and certain places, sights and smells brought her back to him as if she had never left . . .

He was barely twenty when he met her. She was three years his senior but he didn't know that until he was already infatuated. He had been riding around the desert on horseback, happy to have a day off from ranching, when he passed a sand hill and came across a small camp. A horse was tied to a cactus a few feet away from a fire which had been extinguished. A heap of blankets lay next to the old fire and Phil could see a human shape lying under them.

It was noon. Not many cowpokes would let themselves sleep so late into the day, especially out in the open where their unprotected presence was inviting to hostile Indians and bandits. Of course, if the cowpoke in question was sick they might not be able to move themselves out of harm's way. Phil didn't like the idea of leaving a man who might be sick alone and stranded in the middle of nowhere. Tentatively, he approached the figure. If the cowpoke was still alive he'd find out if something was ailing him and, if necessary, bring him to the town doctor immediately.

As he leaned down and extended a hand, he wondered if his good intentions could backfire. Phil wasn't armed, suppose this was a trap and the man under the blankest was a gunman? If he was after his horse Phil would be dead before he could blink . . . yet the idea of leaving a possibly helpless person to die was worse. Swallowing his doubts, Phil shook the sleeping figure. The person under the blankets jumped in surprise at Phil's touch and, before he could finish voicing his "howdy," a young woman was aiming a pistol at his face.

"Don't even think of takin' nothin'," she growled in a slight Mexican accent. "I got nothin' here I can afford to lose an' I'll defend myself an' my belongin's. I ain't got no problem with shootin' a thief."

Phil held his hands up in a surrender position. "I don't mean you no harm, ma'am, but I saw you sleepin' an' I thought you were sick. Not many fellas sleep out in the desert this late in the day."

"I ain't no fella."

"I noticed. What're you doin' sleepin' out here at this time anyway?"

"I was tired. I had a long day yesterday an' I had trouble getting' to sleep last night. I didn't expect to get no visitors this mornin'."

"Actually it's the afternoon," Phil replied, unable to suppress a grin. His hands were still in a surrender posture and he was well aware that his new acquaintance had not lowered her gun. Although he was quite possibly facing death, Phil couldn't keep his eyes off the woman. She was short and small-boned with jet-black hair that hung to her waist. Her large eyes were as rich and dark as the finest chocolate. Her skin was lightly tanned with an olive undertone. He had never seen anyone who looked quite like her.

"You ain't funny," the woman declared, turning her head to hide a smile.

"I ain't a threat either."

"I suppose, you don't look like one anyhow," she replied, finally putting the gun down. "An' it's good to know that you were lookin' to see if I needed help. It's nice to know that some folks still care about others. I'm Darcy Mendez, by the way."

"Phil Palmer. Where you headin' to?"

"Mexico."

"Why you goin' over there?"

"I live there."

"You don't look like most Mexicans I seen."

"My mother was Scottish. I was born in this country but when I was young my mom died an' Papa moved me back over the border to be with his family."

"Why you back here all alone?"

Darcy shrugged. "I speak the best English. My family lives in a poor area. We ain't got much medicine or resources so every month or so I come across the border an' get some supplies. Not just for me, for my whole town."

"Where you get your supplies from?"

"Why you wanna know?"

"I live right around here an' I ain't never seen you in town."

"I go to this place called Cattle Skull. I was born in that town an' I lived there until I was four years old. I'm on good terms with the doctor and the general store owner. They give me food an' medicine for baskets and blankets my grandmother makes."

"I know Cattle Skull well. I got a few friends over there. My pa an' I pass that town on cattle drives. I never saw you there before. I'm from a little town called Dry Heat. It's a lot closer than Cattle Skull an' I'm sure we could spare some supplies for you every now an' then. My uncle's the sheriff; I'll ask him if I can take some extra items from the delivery post. We get tons of extra lanterns an' stuff every now an' then."

"Thanks, it's a kind offer."

"You want help packin'?"

"That'd be nice."

And that was how the relationship between Darcy and Phil began. Phil rode with Darcy to the border, talking all the way, and when they finally bid good-bye Darcy mentioned that she might find an excuse to come back to New Mexico the same time the following week. Phil greatly anticipated their next meeting and over the course of a week he managed to collect two bowls and six candles for her. The following week Darcy arrived right on time and they spent another day riding around the desert chatting like two squirrels in a tree. Before long, Darcy's trips across the border turned from monthly into weekly and then to every two or three days. For over a year, Darcy and Phil met to trade supplies, talk, laugh, and explore the desert. Finally, Darcy's grandmother became suspicious of her granddaughter's endless excuses to leave the country and demanded an explanation for her behavior. After her grandmother threatened to have her horse taken away, Darcy confessed and told her family about Phil. The Mendezs insisted that they meet Phil, and approve of him, or Darcy's trips to the United States would end abruptly.

Phil had been nervous about meeting Darcy's kin. Yet his worrying had been in vain—the Mendezs were a lively, jolly family who readily accepted him into their circle. Phil had never eaten authentic Mexican food before, and Darcy's grandmother knew how to cook well. While in Darcy's home he met Niño, her pet goat. Darcy came from a farming family and a year or so before Phil met her one of the goats on Darcy's farm had forsaken her baby. Not wanting to see the baby goat die, Darcy had taken it upon herself to bottle feed him. Thus the little goat had gotten the name Niño, which meant 'little boy.' Phil knew that Darcy liked animals but it wasn't until he was in her yard helping her feed the chickens, goats, and pigs, that he realized just what a kind touch she had with living creatures.

After visiting Darcy's family, Phil had arranged for her to have dinner at his house. To his delight, his parents liked Darcy just as much as her parents liked him. Over dinner Darcy told his parents about her family, which prompted Phil to suggest that everyone eat a meal together. A month later, when the Palmers and the Mendezes sat down to dinner, the evening had been so much fun that they decided to try to meet for a meal each month. Phil was ecstatic. It was important that the two families get along since he was planning to propose to Darcy on their second anniversary, which was two weeks away. Then the storm came.

The desert didn't get many storms but when it rained, it poured. There had been warning that the storm was coming and everyone was told to stay indoors until the skies cleared. Both Phil and Darcy knew the rain was imminent, and they agreed to wait until the sun was back to meet again. On the night of the storm Phil stayed inside playing cards with his folks, secure in thinking that Darcy was safe at home with her family.

A part of Phil died the next day when Darcy's father

arrived at the Palmers' house weeping uncontrollably. Phil was told that Darcy had been home during the storm. She had been inside the house and safe until a shutter blew open; the quick glance she got out of the window when she went to close it sealed her fate. Niño had somehow managed to get out of the barn and jump the fence. He had lost his footing in the thick mud and was crying for help as he was carried away from the Mendezes' property. Darcy reacted instinctively and ran outside to rescue the goat. Despite her family's pleas for her to come back inside, Darcy disappeared into the dark, wet night.

They found Darcy and the goat the next day. She was lying lifeless in a pool of muddy water. Niño had survived the ordeal and was munching on a cactus approximately twelve feet away from her body. Phil had gone to Darcy's funeral filled with grief so enormous that it turned into rage. Looking at her body Phil had shed an ocean of tears and his mind had shrieked with fury. How could she die? How dare she do this to him! How could she have left him like this all because of a goat— a goat which survived without a scratch while she, the woman he loved, lay dead! Phil had cursed Darcy for her foolishness and her love of animals, which had led to such a cruel death. Behind Phil's anger was a sorrow so vast it filled him with hopelessness. After Darcy died he spent his nights lying awake and his days staring into nothing. He stopped eating and only started again, forcefully, after his mother had cried in front of him and pleaded with him not to let himself die. Slowly,

Phil started working the ranch and sleeping nights again, yet the terrible emptiness inside of him remained.

About eight months after Darcy's death, Phil's Uncle Henry—the infamous sheriff—and his equally infamous deputy were gunned down in a crooked card game. Phil, who had just turned twenty-three, took his uncle's place as sheriff. More than a few townsfolk were wary about allowing any relative of Henry's to become a lawman. Yet, the majority of the town knew and liked Phil and, although young, he made a good sheriff. He appointed a childhood friend named Ira Stacks as deputy and, for nineteen years, the lawmen had some good times together. Then Ira left Dry Heat forever, humiliated after his wife ran off with a coal miner.

And wasn't that the way life always was for Phil? People walked in and out while he stayed alone and the same. Everyone he formed a bond with and cared about left him eventually. Even his folks. They had lived good, long lives before succumbing to old age but that didn't stop Phil from missing them terribly. And then there was Clyde, his big brother, the person he looked up to and thought of as a hero. When Clyde was eighteen and Phil was twelve, Clyde had left Dry Heat to move east. Although they had kept in touch by letters, Phil never saw his brother again in person.

Clyde ended up in New Jersey where he had started a successful business building wagons and carriages. Twenty years after moving, he met and married Marie, an orphan who was his junior by eleven years, and fathered two children late in life. For many years life and correspondence was good, the brothers stayed close friends despite the many miles between them—and then the consumption epidemic hit. Clyde, Marie, and their eleven-year-old son, John, had taken ill and were sent to rest in a sanatorium. Cynthia, blessedly unaffected, was sent to live with a kindly widowed neighbor named Mrs. Baxter.

John died first, then Marie and, knowing his days were numbered, Clyde wrote to his brother. In what was to be his final letter, Clyde asked Phil to look after Cynthia. She had no other family and she couldn't remain with Mrs. Baxter forever. Clyde confessed that he feared Cynthia becoming an orphan. He had heard such heart-wrenching stories from his wife that the very idea of his daughter living such a life was enough to reduce him to tears. Having Phil care for Cynthia was Clyde's dying wish. Clyde ended his letter by telling Phil that although Cynthia had never met him, she had grown up listening to stories about him and reading his letters and she often expressed interest in meeting her cowboy uncle. Apparently, she also looked a great deal like him.

Phil had quickly responded to his brother's letter and immediately agreed to look after Cynthia. He spent hours writing to Clyde, Mrs. Baxter, and Cynthia herself to make the arrangement final. He had wanted to go to New Jersey to collect Cynthia, it didn't seem fair for her to make such a long journey by herself, yet leaving Dry Heat wouldn't have been possible. It was a three-day trip each way, and it would not have been fair to leave Ron in charge for that long.

Thank God I didn't go, the last few days we've been

havin' between cougars an' Hubbards an' storms an' Larry's guys—I'd have come home to chaos.

Although Phil had been quick to promise care for Cynthia, he was more than nervous—he was terrified. Sure, he was her next of kin but he was also a lifelong bachelor who knew nothing about women or children, especially ones scarred by tragedy. He was a gruff, going-on-old man who lived above the town prison. Was that any way for a young girl to grow up? Sometimes Phil cursed Clyde for moving away. Just when everybody was coming west, Clyde, a western-born boy, just had to defy rules and go east. Clyde was always doing things backwards and he had a way of getting on Phil's nerves. Yet, now that he would never see his brother again, Phil regretted all the times they had gotten into sibling spats. He wouldn't think of refusing his brother's dying wish but Phil wondered if the move was in Cynthia's best interest. She was only thirteen years old and she had already watched her mother, father, and brother die. Now she, a city girl, was being transported, all alone, on a train more than halfway across the country and a world away from what she was used to. Phil wanted life in Dry Heat to be good and easy for Cynthia; she had already been through enough grief and pain to last her a lifetime. Yet, he highly doubted his ability to supply her with the ideal life and that thought frightened him. In truth, he was afraid of something happening to her. He didn't want to lose someone again. He had already lost too many people who were close to him.

Phil turned to his side hoping to put his swirling thoughts to rest and get some sleep. Maggie had tried her best to make the floor comfortable by supplying ample blankets, yet a wooden floor provided only half the comfort of a good mattress. That was at least one thing he had done right as far as Cynthia was concerned—he had cleaned out an old room in his house and fully furnished it. His main goal was to make her feel comfortable from the second she arrived. He had gone so far as to buy a brand new doll at the general store and place it on the bed. All little girls liked dolls, didn't they?

"I want to do right by her," Phil whispered, unaware that he was speaking aloud.

You'll be fine, the ghostly voice of Darcy replied. *Everything is goin' to be just fine.*

Although Phil knew those words were empty comfort, and the voice in his head was merely a memory, the reassurance comforted him enough to fall into a deep, dreamless sleep.

According to Blackeye the wind had shifted and the storm had changed. It was now heading northwest, leaving the southeast free of high winds and blowing sand—this was ideal for the Hubbards. All day they had argued about when to start their journey. After spending one night with her family, Katie was ready to ride to town at the crack of dawn, but Gilroy and Blackeye were skeptical. As lifelong bandits who often relied on good weather to survive, both men knew the signs of a dust storm and neither one would agree to ride until they were certain that they were safe from the possibility of such a storm.

"I ain't gettin' my lungs filled with sand because I was rushin' to get revenge on a town I ain't laid eyes on for the best part of ten years!" Gilroy had declared, instigating a shouting match with Katie. Throughout the day the tension between the Hubbards was thick enough to cut with a knife. Yet, late in the afternoon, Blackeye studied the winds and announced that the storm had shifted.

"It ain't a real strong one anyway," he explained. "It'll last maybe a day, ain't gonna last two. If we leave tomorrow mornin' we'll make twenty miles easy, reckon we'll get a decent night's sleep an' all."

Dry Heat was a full fifty miles away from the Hubbard property, yet they had worked out a plan which made Cattle Skull their first destination. Since reuniting with her family, Katie had concocted the perfect revenge plan. Dwayne had known all the town gossip and he had repeated every iota of information he knew to his wife. Katie had never been particularly interested in the lives and times of the townspeople but she did recall Dwayne telling her that the sheriff's orphaned niece was coming to town on Saturday. This information was the basis of her plot.

The Hubbards would leave their home early Friday morning and start riding to Cattle Skull. With luck, they would reach the western outskirts well before dark. Hopefully they would be able to set up camp and get a full night of sleep. On Saturday morning they would wait for the train, ride up to it, hop on board, and subdue the passengers. Blackeye reckoned that slowing the train down would ensure that they would have time to get all the passengers gagged and tied before reaching Dry Heat. Originally Katie had not liked Blackeye's plan. She argued that slowing down the train would alert the waiting sheriff that something was amiss, yet Blackeye saw no such threat. Trains often ran late, especially after a sandstorm which might have damaged or covered the tracks. Katie had to admit that Blackeye was good at thinking things through.

Many Hubbards were participating in this trip. Aside from Gilroy, Blackeye, and Leroy; five other cousins—Danny, Arnold, James, Wallace, and Max—were coming along. Amanda and Roberta had also agreed to help with the ambush; eleven Hubbards in all. The capacity for violence in Hubbard women was nothing new or surprising; they had often robbed and ransacked alongside their men—and they were rarely caught. Roberta was excited about this upcoming mission which she dubbed as "takin' a little vacation." She was looking forward to reaching Dry Heat and looting the stores of anything worth taking.

Katie didn't care what happened to the town goods. She only wanted to get her hands on the girl. Katie planned to kill all the men involved in that ill-fated cougar hunting posse, yet she wanted to make Phil watch as she ended his niece's life. The sheriff had taken Dwayne away from her so she would take his niece away from him, an eye for an eye.

Chapter Thirteen

"Y'all mind them horses now, I already gave you more than I can spare," Maggie declared smiling as she watched the well-rested men prepare to return to town.

It was ten o'clock in the morning. The storm had made way for a picturesque blue sky. Phil was leaving Maggie's house with a stomach full of breakfast and clean clothes on his back. He had been touched to learn that Maggie had not only washed the blood off his shirt, she had also taken time to sew the area which the bullet had ripped.

Although Maggie owned only seven horses she allowed the men to borrow four so everyone but Phil had to double up. Jack and Pete, Clayton and Jonas, and Ron and Sam were paired two to a horse. Before riding into Dry Heat they would return to the coal mines and Phil would use the space on the back of his horse to carry the stolen sacks back to town. It would certainly be interesting to see how the townsfolk reacted to Larry once they discovered he had been stealing from them.

"Thank you," Phil said to Maggie from atop his borrowed horse. He was having trouble balancing himself, as riding a horse other than Crow felt strange. "I'll have these horses returned to you before sundown."

"You better," Maggie retorted in good humor, "an' I hope you'll take the time to stop in here every once in a while. You're always welcome."

"That's a deal, Miss Maggie," he replied, tipping his hat and prodded his horse into a gallop. Leaving Maggie's house was more difficult than he expected; it was like leaving home.

The sand from the storm had covered both the sacks and the bodies, and it took the sheriff and his men a good half hour to locate the stolen goods. It took another ten minutes to drag them back to the horse and securely fasten them atop it.

"What 'bout the bodies?" Clayton asked.

"We'll deal with them later," Phil replied, mounting his horse. He was eager to get back into town and expose Larry as a fraudulent crook.

"Ain't it wrong to just leave 'em out here?" Jonas asked.

"It's the living I'm worried about for now. We need to get on back to town," Phil declared, grappling with the rein.

"I ain't goin' to no town!" Pete cried, panic within his voice.

"We need your help," Phil explained. "If just the two of us lawmen go back there spinnin' the kind of story we're gonna be tellin,' folks will think bein' caught out in that storm has our judgment off. With you outsiders backin' our claim, we have a bigger number of people sayin' the same thing and it might be more believable to folks who wasn't there."

"I ain't no fool an' I ain't goin' in no town!" Pete persisted. "It ain't safe! Towns like yours is death to us!"

"I can't speak for where you come from but I swear that the folks in Dry Heat ain't like that," Ron reassured.

"He's right," Phil continued. "The folks of Dry Heat are good souls an' they ain't even gonna think of harmin' no friends of mine."

"Yo' sure 'bout that? Even if yo' friends are negroes?" Clayton questioned.

"Not if we get to tellin' them what happened before they start askin' us questions. I ain't gonna lie to y'all; we been havin' some trouble with some folks in our town. About a year an' a half ago this fella named Larry Tulmacher rode into our town an' started takin' over. Those are his men lyin' dead under the sand. Tulmacher ain't no nice guy but he can talk mighty sweet an' he's twistin' the mood of our town into somethin' awful. Findin' these sacks is the first real chance I've got to oust this fella, but I need your help to do it."

"Okay, then, you got our help," Jack replied.

"What?" Pete cried in horror, turning to look at the younger man.

"They the only folks who been good to us so far an' if they need our help I ain't gonna refuse 'em," Jack replied before turning to Phil. "You're *sure* that this town is gonna be safe for us, right?"

"It will be perfectly pleasant. Folks there respect us an' if they see y'all are our guests then there ain't gonna be no problem."

"I still ain't sure 'bout this," Pete replied. "If there's any trouble I'm ridin' out, fast."

"That's a deal," Phil replied as he spurred his horse to move toward town, prompting the other men to follow.

Clarence Harden was in a bad mood. He had tried to reason with Carrie. He had offered to save her from the hangman's noose for the price of a courtship and she had responded by spitting in his face. So her fate was decided—she would be hanged for murder. Initially Clarence had not planned to execute the barmaid. However, her brazen rejection of his offer had enraged him to the point where he decided to go through with the execution. If he couldn't have her then no one would.

Clarence watched the hustle and bustle of the town from the front porch of Claire's Cactus. Throughout the morning people had been scurrying around observing the damage the storm had done and waiting to see what would become of Carrie at noon. Clarence was relieved to see Larry feeling better this morning. He was walking around the town talking to all those who passed by him on the street. Aside from Larry, Clarence had not seen any of the other men in their circle, which was unusual.

Them lazy fools are probably still sleepin' off their whiskey, he thought disdainfully. Clarence had never gotten along particularly well with the hard-edged, rough-shaven men Larry had come to town with. They had mean tempers and powerful guns, which Clarence feared winding up on the wrong end of. Yet, despite such unfavorable feelings, he hoped the tougher men would be downstairs by noon in case there was trouble with the barmaid.

Clarence rolled and lit a cigarette before lying back against the rails of the saloon, enjoying the feel of the sun on his face. *At least the lawmen are gone,* he thought, unable to suppress a smile.

There were signs that the sheriff and the deputy wouldn't be coming back. About an hour after the lawmen left town yesterday their horses had come running home without their owners. Less than half an hour later ten more saddled yet riderless horses appeared. Clarence had no idea what had happened near the coal mines but it didn't seem like anything good. Even if the sheriff and the deputy had somehow survived the shootout, it was highly unlikely that they were able to withstand the sandstorm. Clarence had highlighted these facts for Carrie, but she had only put her hands over her ears and screamed until he walked away from her. *Stupid, stubborn woman,* he thought grimacing. It pained him to see such a beautiful woman meet an end like this but it was no harm to him; he supposed the Doherty girl would make a good enough match after all.

I reckon that I'll become sheriff if Palmer don't come back, Clarence thought happily. Oh yes, once Larry was mayor and Rombert was just another drunk in the bar, Clarence would be the sheriff. When Larry passed on, he would assume the position of mayor. Clarence Harden was moving up in the world, he was going to be successful! Who cared about what happened on that jailkeeping job three years ago? He was aiming for the mayor's office now!

The sound of galloping horses heading toward him snapped Clarence out of his thoughts. He supposed he shouldn't have been surprised when he saw the sheriff and the deputy arrive at the front of the saloon but he couldn't mask his disappointment—nor could he hide his horror when he saw the five black faces who accompanied the lawmen.

"Howdy, Clarence," the sheriff said solemnly, "is Larry around?"

"I saw your horses come back! How'd y'all survive that storm an' where did *they* come from?" His voice was rising, his finger pointed toward the black cowboys.

"We had us quite a day an' met some interestin' folks," Ron replied. "Now go get Larry."

"I don't got to take orders—"

"Well, if it ain't the lawmen!" Larry boomed merrily, emerging from the doorway of Claire's Cactus. "I ain't seen you all day an' . . ." His smile vanished and his words dried up as soon as he spotted the five ex-slaves. "Where'd *they* come from?" he shouted, sounding angrier than Phil had ever heard him.

"We found 'em in the desert."

"I told y'all about their sort!" Larry screamed hysterically, garnering the attention of half the town. "I warned y'all time an' time again. I told you not to let 'em step one foot in this town, I—"

"You're a thief," Phil interrupted calmly.

"What?" Larry asked. There was a noticeable edge in his voice, and he looked uncharacteristically nervous. He was well aware of the large group of townspeople gathering to watch the spectacle.

"You know what we're talkin' about," Phil replied, fixing Larry with a cold gaze.

"How could I steal? I've been in my room most of the night with a fever!"

"Really, or were you just takin' some time up there to pack your bags? You were plannin' on movin' out of here with your ill-gotten gains an' movin' on to the next town as soon as the storm ended, weren't you?"

"What ill-gotten gains? What're you talkin' about?"

Phil reached back, unfastened a sack, and threw it onto the ground by Larry's feet. The townspeople gasped as the sack opened and its shiny contents spilled forth. The golden nuggets gleamed in the sun, the bills rustled in the wind, and Larry looked like he had just been shot.

"It's funny that you should have all this gold right about this time. Wasn't it just about a week ago that you got the key to the town? You know, that big old skeleton key that opens every vault in the bank? Willis gave it to you right in front of this town as a token of appreciation an' look at what you done with all that respect you had. It's over, Larry. Your men are dead an' collecting sand up near them mines. As soon as we're done with you we gotta bury their bodies," Phil added, enjoying the look of fear on the politician's face.

Larry had broken into a sweat. He was looking from the sheriff, to the gold, to the townspeople with eyes as wide as an owl's. Yet it was Clarence who was truly confused. Larry's entire posse was dead? Scotch, Jabs, Bryant, Red, and Ropes were all gone? And what was this talk about Larry stealing all the money out of the bank? Clarence reckoned that once Larry was mayor there would be some fiddling with the funds but nothing this bad.

It can't be true, Clarence thought. *Larry wouldn't rob this town, he's been here a full year an' he's sure to become mayor! He wouldn't leave. He ain't got no reason to. An' then there's me! I've helped him a lot since he came here an' he promised he'd help me gain power in this town. He wasn't lyin', couldn't be, not after all that work I put in! He won't leave, he won't. They're just tryin' to get under our skin.*

"Most of that gold's from the creek," Phil announced to the townspeople. "That's the gold a vast number of you worked your hands to the bone for. An' he was just gonna up an' take it from y'all."

"I darn near killed myself searchin' that creek!" an

angry voice rose from the crowd, prompting an uprising of outrage.

"He came real close to gettin' away with it," Phil continued. "You got the folks behind me to thank for stoppin' him. They saw his men hidin' the sacks in the mines before the storm. That's what all the shootin' was about. Larry's friends were lookin' to kill these men for what they saw."

"An' that's de Lord's truth," Jonas replied.

"Are y'all gonna listen to this?" Larry roared, pointing at Jonas but looking at the townspeople. "I've been warnin' y'all about their kind since I got here! Now a couple of 'em come around these parts an' a couple of us wind up dead. Don't that seem strange to none of you? Can't you see what's happenin' here? The sheriff an' the deputy are helpin' 'em, figurin' that they can get rid of me an' stop the changes that need to be made to this town, good changes! Look at your sheriff, his uncle wasn't no great man, what makes you think he's any better? Corruption is in his blood!"

"You think we wanted to go out in that storm?" Phil shouted at the town's populace, feeling as if he had been slapped in the face. "We only went out because we thought somebody was in trouble. Heck, a few kids from town were the ones who told us what was goin' on! I've been a sheriff for a long time an' I ain't never done you no wrong. My uncle was a poor excuse for a man, I'm the first to admit that, but I ain't nothin' like him an' y'all know it."

The townspeople were mumbling amongst each other

and looking from Phil to Larry. Finally, Clarence raised his voice. "I ain't surprised by none of it," he declared. "These lawmen are capable of anything. I mean, look at the company they keep, especially the deputy. Bring out the girl!"

The two large cowpokes that Clarence shouted at were so hypnotized by the unfolding scene that the preacher's son had to smack them to get their attention. Immediately, they went into Claire's Cactus and emerged a few moments later dragging Carrie behind them. She was obviously terrified—kicking, screaming, and crying while pleading for her life, yet when she saw Ron she managed to form a small, desperate smile.

"Let her go!" Ron ordered Clarence, his hand moving toward his gun.

"I ain't gonna do no such thing. Even if you shoot me, there's tons of folks here who'll take care of this murderess."

"What do you mean murderess?" Phil asked, startled.

With a mean-spirited grin on his face Clarence recounted the story of Carrie and the drunk. He made sure to emphasize the drunk being harmless and Carrie cruelly pushing him down the stairs for fun.

"He didn't stand no kinda chance against her," Clarence explained. "He was a frail, old fella. We moved his body into the cellar; you can go take a look if you don't believe me."

"Ron, it ain't true, I swear it ain't!" Carrie screamed, still being held tightly by her captors. "He was grabbin' at me an' tryin' to get into my private room! I was scared an' ran an' he followed. I just wanted him to leave me alone; I didn't want him to go fallin' down them stairs like that! You got to believe me, I ain't been no trouble so far!"

"I believe her," Phil proclaimed. "An' as sheriff I got the top say in this matter, Clarence. Now let her go."

"But you weren't here when she pushed that poor man!" Amelia shrieked, emerging from within the crowd to have her say. "When y'all were out of town this trollop committed a cold-blooded murder! I saw it myself. She deserves to hang an' the whole town agrees."

"Do y'all really?" Ron roared, furious. No one responded. Even Peggy Cobwey was too shaken by the tense mood in the air to state her support of Carrie.

"Well, how do you expect these folks to support anyone who brings the kinda company you do into their town?" Larry snapped, shooting Jack, Jonas, Clayton, Samuel, and Pete a deadly look. Again there was no response uttered from the people of Dry Heat. It was as if a plague of silence had engulfed the entire town.

"I challenge you to a shootout!" Ron announced suddenly, staring hatefully at Clarence.

"You want to have a shootout over a barmaid?" Clarence sneered.

"Yes, an' if I win she goes free."

"I accept your challenge, Deputy, but I reckon you just signed both you an' your lady friend's death certificate."

"Clear out! We need room!" Ron shouted at the townspeople as he dismounted his horse.

Phil and the black cowboys followed his lead. If there

was going to be a shootout they didn't want to take the chance of sitting on a horse that could get spooked. As Phil dismounted he caught Willis' eye. Once on the ground he approached the banker and ordered him to go check the vaults. For once, Willis obeyed without hesitation or complaint.

Realizing that Ron was putting his life on the line, both Peggy and Carrie felt their stomachs turn in knots. Amelia seemed more interested in the unfolding events than concerned about Clarence. She was smirking hatefully at Carrie, obviously anticipating seeing her hang. Preacher Warren watched the scene with a growing sense of dread. He feared that this time his nephew had gone too far.

Clarence and Ron stood ten feet apart. The tension in the air was so thick it was almost smothering. For the first time in a while Phil was truly frightened. Was this to be the day he lost another friend? Despite the sick feeling in the pit in his stomach, Phil called the countdown.

"One . . . two . . . three . . . draw!"

Clarence went for his gun first but Ron was quicker. Two shots rang out within milliseconds of each other. One bullet missed Ron's head by less than an inch. The other bullet flew squarely into Clarence's chest. Instantly, the preacher's nephew fell dead upon the ground. Before the dust had cleared from Clarence's toppled frame, Willis came running out of the bank waving his arms in the air and shrieking hysterically. "Everything's gone! The vault's been robbed clean; ain't nothin' left!"

"An' Larry's got all his bags packed," a gruff-voiced

woman declared. Phil turned and saw Claire standing on the porch of her saloon holding the politician's large suitcase.

"Is he dead?" Warren Harden wailed from the ground where he was cradling his nephew's body in his arms. Dr. Noonan was crouched beside him searching in vain for a pulse. Instead of answering the distraught preacher's question, the doctor nodded and patted his back. Not wanting to intrude on Warren's grief, Phil turned his attention towards Larry.

"I reckon it's time for you to go," Phil declared as Warren prayed over his nephew's body and Carrie ran into Ron's arms.

"I ain't gotta go nowhere."

"Oh, you better," Peggy growled. "You've proven what kind of man you are an' it's high time you get your sorry hide out of here. I ain't pleased to call a drunk the mayor of my town but I'd rather a drunk than a thief! We're just workin' folks an' you gained our trust only to rob us blind. I don't want a man like you nowhere near my town!"

Larry stared at the angry faces which surrounded him, seemingly helpless for the first time. Stripped of his power, he stared at the townspeople with real fear and, noting that Jack, Clayton, Jonas, Pete, and Samuel were there to witness his downfall, rage.

"I lost everythin' in the war," he hissed, "everything. I used to have wealth so vast it would shame a king, an' after the war I was reduced to nothin' above a beggar. It ain't right."

"An' it ain't right to prey on folks who have less than you do," Phil replied. "Now you best be getting out of this town. Normally a thief like you would be strung up—tarred and feathered at least—but this town's seen too much violence in the past week so I'm gonna make you a deal. If you get outta here within the next ten minutes I'll make sure nobody raises a hand to you. Just pick up your bag, get on your horse, an' get away from us. I'd throw you in jail but then I'd have to look at your miserable hide all day an' neither I nor my deputy done nothin' to deserve that."

Plus, I don't want you to get a chance at weaslin' your way out from behind bars somehow. Phil didn't want to deal with a jailed Larry, he just wanted him out of town—forever. Larry glared at Phil hatefully one final time before grabbing his suitcase and heading toward the corral.

"Y'all are a bunch of thievin' liars!" Amelia screamed at the lawmen. "Y'all set up Larry an' poor Clarence to let that murderin' little tramp walk free! There ain't no justice in this town!"

"I agree!" Adeline shrieked, coming to her daughter's defense. "Y'all have traumatized my babies with all the shootin' an' murderin'!"

"This ain't no kind of place to find a husband!" Edwina announced, sharing her mother's and sister's views on the town.

"Now that Larry," Adeline continued, "there's a man who could have taken care of all this mess. There's a man who could have set things straight if y'all didn't go framin' him! Well, if he goes, we go! An' you, Deputy Harris, are the biggest fool I ever did meet!"

With that said, the three Doherty women marched back to their house and packed their few belongings. Within a half hour they had mounted their horses and rode out of Dry Heat. As the Dohertys rode off into the sunset after Larry, Ron and Carrie shared their first kiss.

Chapter Fourteen

It was three-thirty in the afternoon on the following day. The Saturday mail train had been due to arrive at one o'clock and Phil had left at noon to ensure he would be at the station just in case it came early. Ron snickered as he imagined the impatient sheriff waiting the extra hours at the station.

I knew it wasn't gonna come early, Ron thought, *especially after a sandstorm. Poor old Phil's probably sittin' there playin' solitaire an' cussing that train to Satan under his breath.*

Phil had left Ron in charge while he rode a half mile to the train station in order to collect Cynthia. Ron had spent the early afternoon lending a helping hand to folks who were tidying up the mess the storm had made to their homes and shops. He had also paid his respect to

Warren Harden, who had buried Clarence that morning. Unsurprisingly, the funeral had been scarcely attended.

Ron felt as if the events of the last few days were part of some strange dream. He couldn't believe that Larry and the Dohertys were gone. Nor could he believe that he had killed Clarence in a shootout and saved Carrie's life. Although she was unharmed physically, the stress of the day before had made Carrie feel weak. She was resting under the caring eyes of the Cobweys and, it seemed, she was prepared to be courted by Ron, which made him feel fresh with joy.

He and Phil had captivated the townspeople with their tale of survival via Maggie and her Indian family. The townspeople had been both enthralled and disbelieving that the woman they regarded as insane was the reason that the sheriff and the deputy had survived. Phil promised to bring Maggie into town within the next few days so the people of Dry Heat could see that she was a sweet, friendly woman—not the crazed witch she was rumored to be.

After realizing that Larry was a lying crook, the majority of the people in Dry Heat had made an immediate effort to be friendly to Jack, Clayton, Samuel, Jonas, and Pete. Although there had been some initial tension based on the lies Larry had spewed, the people had been hospitable to the five ex-slaves. Claire had given them room and board—ironically in the same rooms Larry and his men had inhabited—for minimum cost, and Peggy had cooked them a full dinner. Although the ex-slaves had been wary about staying in the town, the offer of warm beds and full meals won them over. Ron was pleased. He liked the men and hoped that they would stay in town for a while. It seemed as if they had survived some rough times in the South and deserved peace.

Ron was expecting to have a calm and incident-free day. He was looking forward to an equally pleasant evening when he would finally get to meet Cynthia and spend more time with Carrie. And so, when he saw Sheriff Andy McDowde and Deputy Carl Tillman of Cattle Skull ride up in front of the sheriff's office, Ron was downright flabbergasted. They had obviously been riding hard for a long time. Ron felt pity just looking at their exhausted horses. This was not a card game visit; from the pinched expressions on the men's faces it was obvious that something was wrong. Dreading whatever news they were about to bring, Ron walked out to the front porch and greeted the lawmen.

"I wasn't expectin' to see y'all today," Ron declared.

"We wasn't expectin' to come, we got trouble," Sheriff McDowde replied, looking at Ron tensely, his usually serene brown eyes alert with worry.

"What kind of trouble?" Ron asked with unease creeping into the pit of his stomach.

"We ain't sure yet," Deputy Tillman replied. He was only slightly younger than Andy but he was half the weight and had half the eyesight.

"Awful long way to come if you ain't sure what the problem is or if you even got a problem."

"Well it's about the mail train," Carl explained. "About two hours ago it stopped in our town. It was a little late but it made its stop an' there wasn't nothin' funny reported. Anyway, about a half hour after it left a rancher came ridin' into town all in a huff 'cause he said he saw a bunch of folks on horseback ride up to it an' hop on that train. He said that he couldn't be sure but he thought that it was slowin' down in the distance. He reckoned that it was a strange enough sight to tell us about an' we rode out to investigate. Sure enough the train was slowin' down by a lot—we was goin' faster than it on horseback! I reckon that it coulda been because of sand on the tracks, y'all got that storm stronger than we did, but still somethin' seemed wrong. We reckoned that it was worth tellin' you about, at least get your assistance. There wasn't no use in the two of us approachin' that train alone if somethin' bad is happenin'."

"I've known Phil a long time," Andy added, "we go way back, an' when I heard the news about the train I dang near died. That's the train his niece is on, ain't it?"

"Yes," Ron replied dryly.

Andy nodded solemnly. "Maybe we shoulda rode on over an' asked the engineer if everythin' was allright. We got a few reports sayin' that yesterday's storm knocked out the telegraph line, so even if they was havin' a problem they couldn't report it. But I just got a hunch that comin' over this way was better. After all, that train's comin' past this stop no matter what's goin' on inside it. I reckon that havin' you an' Phil on our side before makin' any rash decisions is the safe way to play this an'

I'm sure Phil would respect the power of hunches. I don't like to say this but I have a feelin' that if somethin' bad is goin' on it has to do with Cynthia. We've had a few ranchers movin' cattle from town to town this past week an' you know how much folks like to talk. We heard all about that cougar scare an' what happened with that Hubbard woman's husband last week. You think she could be plannin' somethin'? Them folks always was a bad lot."

Ron stared at Andy. Of course, Katie! She was hateful and deranged and it would be just like a Hubbard to cause trouble for the sake of twisted vengeance.

"She's after Cynthia," Ron declared horrorstruck. "Phil's at the station waitin' for her now! We need to warn him before it's too late."

Ron was hastily saddling up Nita when Jack approached the corral.

"It's nice to have your own horse back ain't it?" Jack declared pleasantly. "It was mighty nice of that woman to give us her horses but there ain't nothin' like havin' yo' own."

Suddenly, Jack noticed the tension-filled look on Ron's face.

"Is there a problem, Deputy?"

"It seems that way."

"If yo' spare a minute an' tell me what the problem be I might be able to help."

Ron hesitated only for a moment before telling Jack everything the Cattle Skull lawmen had told him. "If

Katie is responsible for this then we have a big problem," he concluded.

"I know yo' in a rush to get the sheriff," Jack replied as
he backed away from the corral, "but if yo' spare a few
minutes me an' the others will come wit y'all. It sounds
like yo' need all the help yo' can get."

Jack was running to get his friends before Ron had
time to utter a response. He hated to waste another second but maybe the few extra men would come in handy.
Nine men were better than four, especially if Katie's
family was involved.

Ron recapped the events of the past few days, and the
presence of the black cowboys, to the Cattle Skull lawmen. Once Jack, Jonas, Clayton, Samuel, and Pete had
their horses, the eight men rode to the station to warn
Phil of the danger ahead.

When Jack heard the lawmen of Dry Heat needed
help, the thought of withholding aid never crossed his
mind. Jack and his four companions had not lived easy
lives. Jack, like his four friends, had been born into
slavery and never got the opportunity to know his family. Whenever he grew close to someone that person
was eventually separated from him via death or sales,
and so from a young age he had known great loneliness. He had spent his life working his hands to the
bone with nothing but scars to show for it. When the
war had begun, he had escaped his master to join the
Union Army—as much for the promise of daily rations
as the possibility of freedom. He had seen such horrific

battles that he wished his mind could erase the memories. After the war, he had his freedom but he was scorned in most places, causing him to fear for his life on a daily basis. He wandered aimlessly around the country for a few years and, during that time, he met fellow drifters Jonas, Clayton, Samuel, and Pete. They had all decided that going west to California would be the best—the safest—way to start over and find a new life of peace.

Moving west had been both a blessing and a trial; they had been free from the fear their hometowns offered, yet the further they rode into the desert, the more cut off and alone they became. They had battled unbearably hot days and bone chillingly cold nights; they had survived the sudden rains and vicious sandstorms, yet they dared never to enter a town, fearing hostilities. They had been lonely wanderers who were wounded by their pasts and haunted by the memories of those who they had loved and befriended—those who they had somehow lost. Jack reckoned that it had been a stroke of unbelievably good luck that they had been at just the right place, at just the right time, to have crossed paths with the Dry Heat lawmen. The people of Dry Heat had been the first to show kindness and compassion toward Jack and his comrades. Dry Heat was the first place which felt like a home.

Jack felt that he and his friends owed the sheriff loyalty in return for his kindness and, noting how quickly his four companions had geared up their horses at the mention of trouble, it seemed that they felt the same.

Jack wasn't exactly sure what he and his friends were getting themselves into, but if this Katie Hubbard woman was looking to cause the sheriff or the town trouble, then Jack was more than willing to step in and stop her.

Playing solitaire and cradling a sore arm was hard, but anything was better than the mind-numbing boredom of an empty train station on a hot day. Phil wasn't the only man there—whenever the train came in it was a big event for the town merchants who had taken to standing in the corner smoking and telling raunchy jokes. Phil was in no mood to joke or smoke and so he sat silently by himself.

If I hadn't brought these cards I'd have killed myself by now, he thought grumpily as he glanced at the clock on the wall. Wade Horace, the station's one employee, was trying to fix the telegraph box. From the amount of foul language filling the air, Phil reckoned Wade wasn't having much luck.

"How much longer you reckon this train's gonna take?" Phil called.

"How should I know?" Wade snapped, sticking his head out of his office door. "This dang thing ain't workin' so I got no way to tell what's goin' on. I reckon the whole system's out, not just my machine. An' that storm yesterday probably wrecked havoc on the tracks, sand drifts are everywhere! Trains are always late after storms. Hold your horses, Sheriff, it'll get here."

"Sure," Phil replied as he gathered his cards and placed the pack into the right front pocket of his shirt.

He stood and paced the room to stretch his legs, feeling like a kid cooped up in a classroom. Aside from the general boredom of waiting, Phil's anxiousness was eating up his insides. He was worried about the train being late but he was even more nervous about finally meeting his niece. Phil was deep in thought about what he would do if Cynthia didn't like him when Ron and the other men burst into the station. Their sudden entry made Wade scream and Phil and the waiting merchants jump.

"We got trouble, Phil!" Andy exclaimed, before telling Phil everything that had happened.

"An' it looks like its good we got here," Carl added, glancing at Wade and the telegraph box. "Them things ain't workin' in our town neither, so that train's got no way to call for help."

"It could be slow because of the storm," Phil declared, praying and hoping against hope that nothing really bad was happening on the train.

"Or it could have intentionally slowed down for some reason," Ron added.

"Or both," Carl declared solemnly.

"We think this could be Katie's doin'," Ron explained. "It sounds like somethin' she'd do if she went back an' got her family to come an' help her. She's got a ton of kin an' them folks are always lookin' for trouble. You know how they thrive on revenge. If they're on that train, they're up to no good."

"Let's go now, all of you!" Phil demanded, deeply disturbed by the news he was hearing. "We can start ridin' to that train now. It ain't great that we're goin' toward it head on but we ain't got no choice. There ain't no time to waste; I don't want a train full of bodies pullin' into this station because we were too slow to get to it."

"Can . . . can I do anything to help?" Wade asked tentatively from the doorway of his office.

"Yeah," Phil replied, pointing to the telegram machine. "The second that thing works again alert any local town lawmen—besides Dry Heat and Cattle Skull—that we need reinforcements."

"What about us?" Tommy Maddenson, the town's candlemaker asked. "Is there anythin' we can do? Do y'all need more men?"

"No, you ain't armed so it's too dangerous. Just get on back to town an' tell everyone to be prepared. It looks like the Hubbards might be payin' us a visit."

Wade nodded dutifully and disappeared back into his office as the town merchants headed outside to retrieve their horses. Phil and his eight compadres mounted their horses and rode toward the train, praying they would arrive before it was too late.

Chapter Fifteen

Blackeye had been a thief for a long time. He had robbed dozens of towns; he had gunned down anyone who presented a problem for him, and he had even survived losing an eye to angry Apaches. His life of crime had been prosperous due to good planning and fair luck but never before had anything gone this smoothly. They had made excellent time reaching Cattle Skull and were now awake and alert after a full night's sleep under a clear, starry sky. They had boarded the train without a hitch and easily subdued the passengers. Possibly the best stroke of luck was that the storm had knocked out the telegraph system so the train engineer had no way to call for help. Still, Blackeye liked to play things safe and so he had broken the train's telegraph box despite its temporary uselessness.

He supposed that he would eventually miss the horses

which had ran off as he and his criminal gang jumped onto the train, but losing the horses was part of the plan. They would get to the Dry Heat station, kill the sheriff, the station manager, and any others who happened to be waiting there, and take their horses to ride into town.

Katie had found the sheriff's niece almost immediately and wasted no time in subduing the girl. Although Blackeye had demanded that all the hostages, aside from the engineer who he was holding at gunpoint in the engine room, be gagged, tied, and thrown into the passenger car, Katie made it clear that she was not going to let Cynthia out of her sight. Once Katie got a hold of Cynthia she lost interest in all else and retreated to the engineer's sleeping car—the most comfortable place on the train—to wait out the journey to Dry Heat.

The other hostages, crammed uncomfortably into the passenger car, were being looked over by Leroy, Amanda, and Roberta. Blackeye thanked his lucky stars that this was a mail and supply train instead of a busy city passenger line. All and all, staff and passengers combined, Blackeye assumed that he had a little less than fifty people at his mercy. They were quiet hostages and easy to control and that gave Danny, Arnold, James, Wallace, and Max the opportunity to raid the train. They grabbed goods heading to general stores and stole any items of value they found, including breaking into the train's safe and taking every penny within it. As an afterthought, they forced the hostages to hand over any jewelry they wore.

Indeed, everything was going well for the Hubbards. So far the biggest dilemma was the sand which had blown onto the tracks. Although slowing down the train until the hostages were in control was part of the plan all along, the sand on the tracks was forcing the train to move at little more than a creep—much slower than Blackeye had ever intended to go. In one spot a sand drift was so thick that Blackeye had ordered Amanda, Roberta, and Gilroy—all cussing and protesting—out with a shovel to clear the area. It was slow going but Blackeye saw no harm in the late timing. Folks would be expecting the train to come in late and there was no reason to be alarmed—after all, they weren't getting any distress messages from the telegraph.

Blackeye smiled, exposing a mouth full of rotting teeth. The engineer was a small, timid man—the sort of fellow that Blackeye thought of as an inexcusable coward. As long as Blackeye kept a gun pointed in his general direction the engineer did what he was told. The engineer was the kind of hostage Blackeye liked—heck, this whole plan was the kind he liked—easy to deal with.

Sitting down on a large sack of mail, Blackeye stole a quick glance out the window where the late afternoon sun was setting the desert on fire with its radiant golden glow. Although he rarely showed affection or compassion for anything, he had to admit that he loved the desert landscape and the wild, free life it offered. There was no city in which he could have maintained his criminal status for as long as he had. Cities had large units of lawmen, fast-traveling news, and close communities. In cities it was easy to get caught and sent to prison. Yet the desert was different; it was spacious and wide and hard traveling. It was easy to steal from desert drifters and wagons trains or even the rare lone Indian without having to worry about retribution. Over the years, Blackeye had experienced numerous adventures. He had killed a vulture and cooked its meat when there was a food shortage. He had camped out in an abandoned fort on the Mexican border during a rainstorm, and he had made money rigging more than a few card games. He had survived shootouts and barroom brawls and hostile Indians. He had fought off bats in caves and scorpion bites on the range. He had killed many men, and he reckoned that he knew where more bodies were buried than any man alive. Of course, he didn't know exactly what had happened to everyone he had ever robbed; unless his victim was armed he rarely bothered to shoot them—except if he thought they could identify him to lawmen.

Although he had forgotten many robberies, there were still some cases that stuck out in his mind. Once, not too far from the train's current course, Blackeye had come across a sleeping Chinese man who happened to have a perfectly good mare in his possession. The foreigner had been so deep in sleep that he had not heard Blackeye approach his camp. One glance at the thin, ragged man told his story: He was, or had been, a railway worker. He had probably grown tired of the hard labor and low wages, stolen somebody's horse, and took off. Blackeye had tried to untie the horse and lead it away without waking the man, but the second he approached the horse the man awoke. He wasn't armed but he had lunged at Blackeye, screaming in a language the bandit didn't understand. Blackeye's gun was in its holster and, as he grabbed for it, he knocked the man back with his arm. The smaller man fell over a rock, instantly breaking his leg. Blackeye had been planning to shoot the man, but when he realized that his leg was broken and that he could no longer fight, he decided to leave him alive. It would be a longer, crueler death out in the desert and any man who dared to fight with Blackeye Crawdrum deserved such a fate. The man had remained on the ground, holding his leg and watching helplessly as Blackeye took off with his horse. Although Blackeye hadn't felt guilty about taking the animal—which was probably stolen in the first place— he had often wondered about the fate of that Chinese man. How long had it taken him to die? Had anyone ever found his body? Not that it mattered, that encounter had occurred over thirty years ago. By now that foreigner was nothing but a long-dead bundle of bones lying somewhere in the desert.

Blackeye smiled cruelly as he considered every crime he had managed to get away with over the years. This train hijacking business was turning out to be one of his most successful plots yet. Hijacking and robbing a train, killing a sheriff and his niece, and robbing a town all in one day! If this didn't put him down in criminal folklore history then he didn't know what would. Blackeye chuckled as he considered the enormity of his crimes and thought about what the campfire songs written about him would sound like.

Cynthia sat on the floor of the engineer's sleeping car shaking uncontrollably. Her hands and feet were tied with rope and her mouth was gagged with a handkerchief, which stifled both screams and sobs. Katie was standing over the girl pointing a pistol at her face and ranting about everything from sand storms to her family to her dead husband. She was annoyed by the very presence of the girl who had been the most difficult passenger to control. Cynthia was unexpectedly feisty and she had ran from Katie only to be subdued when Amanda stepped in to help. Cynthia had scratched and screamed, kicked and cried. She hit Amanda with her suitcase and bit Katie on the arm. One quick punch on the lip was what it took to shock Cynthia into passive silence, and Katie was happy to have dealt the blow that shut Cynthia up and bruised her pretty little lips. Every time Katie raised her voice and waved her weapon, Cynthia uttered a muted sob, and each time Katie looked at Cynthia her rage flared.

Cynthia *did* look like her uncle, the resemblance was uncanny. They had the same angular bone structure, the same hazel eyes, and the same shade of thick brown hair. Every time Katie glanced at Cynthia she thought of the sheriff, and that made her remember Dwayne and how he had been so cruelly murdered. Katie wanted the train to get to Dry Heat; she wanted to shoot Cynthia, then the sheriff, and then get into town and take care of that annoying little deputy. Yet, in the meantime, Katie shouted at Cynthia to alleviate her restlessness. It felt good to make the girl quiver with fear the same way her uncle and his cronies had probably made Dwayne quiver before they killed him. The more panicked and hysterical the little brat was when Phil saw her during the last few seconds of her life, the better.

"Your uncle's a bad man," Katie informed Cynthia. "He killed my husband, you know. It's true, he went an' he got a whole posse of men an' they killed my husband with a snake's venom. Ain't it nice to know what sorta man you gonna have lookin' after you?"

The small sob Cynthia gave in response was music to Katie's ears. As long as she had her gun and patience, vengeance would be hers in less than an hour.

I'll get 'em for you, Dwayne honey, she thought as she cradled her husband's memory within her mind, *I'll make sure they pay for what they done to you.*

Gilroy was shoveling coal and Roberta was minding the hostages alongside Leroy and Amanda when Blackeye gave a furious scream from within the engineer's office.

"Stay here," Roberta ordered her daughter and nephew. "I'll go see what the problem is."

When Roberta entered the engine room Gilroy was already there, covered in soot and holding the metal shovel he had found in the coal engine room. In the presence of his captors the engineer trembled. Roberta fixed him with a contemptuous look; cowards irked her more than anything else.

"We got company," Blackeye declared, pointing toward the desert on the other side of the smoky-glass window. It took Roberta a moment to see the outline of a group of men on horseback riding toward the train.

"I'd bet my remainin' eye one of 'em is Phil Palmer," Blackeye growled.

"That dang sheriff is mighty fast to act," Roberta hissed. "How'd he find out about this anyway?"

"I don't know an' I don't care!" Gilroy shouted. "I say we just lean out the window an' start shootin' at 'em; we ain't goin' that fast so our aim should be okay."

"Don't!" Blackeye commanded fiercely. "If y'all start shootin' from here the gunshots could be heard in the distance an' reinforcements could show up. That's one chance I ain't takin'! Let 'em board an' we'll take 'em out in here where the walls will stifle the sound of the blasts. One of you wait for 'em to hop on, they'll probably take the entrance closest to this engine room, an' the other one of you go warn the others we got company—especially Katie. She's got what the sheriff wants most."

In all his years as a lawman, Phil had never before needed to jump from a galloping horse onto a moving train. His stomach was in knots as he turned Crow into a U-turn, forcing him to run adjacent to the train. He was trying desperately not to look down since he knew he would have to time his jump perfectly. Although the train was moving relatively slow, if he didn't time the jump correctly he could lose a leg under the tracks or lose his life under the hooves of his following posse's horses. *I could die right here,* he thought, somewhat frightened. *If I mess the jump, this is the end.*

If you don't jump, Cynthia will die, the voice of Darcy replied firmly.

With those words ringing in his mind, Phil swallowed his fear, braced himself, and leaped toward the moving train. For a few terrifying moments he was suspended in midair, sure he was going to fall to a painful death, and then he was grasping the railing on the inside of the doorway stairs. Happy to be alive, he quickly pulled himself into the train and unholstered his gun. He was aware of his posse boarding the train behind him and running up the stairs after him until they reached a room filled with ransacked bags of mail. Phil barely had time to register his surroundings when Gilroy ran out of the back room of the train and lunged at him holding a metal shovel. Instinctively, Phil fired at his attacker. The bullet ricocheted off the shovel and flew into the wall near the door, missing Deputy Carl Tillman's head by half an inch. Phil ran toward Gilroy and tried to pry the shovel out of his hands.

"I can deal with him! Y'all spread out, find the rest of 'em an' Cynthia!" Phil screamed at his posse as he tussled with Gilroy. The group split and obediently moved toward the back of the train; all but Andy who stayed to help Phil with Gilroy.

"Drop the weapon, Gilroy," Andy demanded, pointing his gun toward the old Hubbard. "Nobody's got to get hurt here."

A bullet suddenly flew past Phil's right side. He looked up to see Roberta standing, gun in hand, near the door to what he assumed was the engine room. "Dang it, Gilroy! You shoulda gone back an' warned the others like you was told to do. I coulda taken care of these two vermin myself," she hissed, aiming to fire another bullet at the two sheriffs.

At the sight of her, Andy returned fire. As soon as the Cattle Skull sheriff started shooting at Roberta, she let out a hail of gunfire that riddled the walls of the train with hot lead. Gilroy used the distraction to swing the shovel at Phil. The metal banged against Phil's head with such force that he saw stars. He resisted the urge to black out but was unable to help falling to the ground, dazed. The next thing he knew Gilroy had his hands wrapped around his throat, determined to squeeze the life out of him.

"I knew I shoulda raided that town an' killed you years ago," Gilroy hissed as he tightened his grip. "Today I'm makin' up for that mistake."

Phil was getting woozy and he couldn't breathe. His lungs were screaming for air and his wounded head was pounding furiously. Thinking of the destruction the Hubbards were planning to unleash upon Dry Heat in a matter of hours, Phil used his last bit of strength to make a grab for the shovel. He was able to grip it but only for a few seconds; his fingers lacked the strength to pick it up.

He was sure he was going to die as he gasped for breath, feeling as trapped as a caged canary in a coal mine. Then, suddenly, Gilroy lost his grip on the sheriff's neck and fell forward, his face twisted into a mask of pain and surprise. Phil's windpipe opened as he thanked God for his spared life. It took him a few seconds to realize that he was covered in Gilroy's blood and Roberta was screaming. Apparently, one of her bullets had bounced off the wall and shot her own husband dead.

"Look at what y'all made me do!" Roberta half screamed, half wailed, before shooting bullets in every direction and shrieking wildly. Phil and Andy hit the floor to avoid the flying lead. Phil's ears were ringing painfully. Wishing for the bullet blasts and screaming woman to be silenced, he grabbed his gun, aimed, and pulled the trigger. It was the sort of perfect shot Phil used to be known for in his younger days. A half second after he fired his weapon, Roberta Hubbard fell to the ground next to her husband, dead. Andy and Phil stood and looked at the bodies of Katie's parents and then at one another. The area that had been filled with gunfire and enraged screaming just seconds before was now eerily silent and hazy with gunsmoke.

We've lost so much money worth of ammo this week that savin' the bank's gold is just gonna let us break even, Phil thought bizarrely. He was often unable to think of anything besides the amount of lost ammo in the moments after a gunfight. Then the train stopped. The sudden halt caused the carriage to lurch forward, sending Phil and Andy tumbling.

From the inside of the engine room Blackeye had listened to the gunfight. Originally he had not ordered the train stopped because he had held out some hope that the sheriff and his men would fall to their deaths as they attempted to board the moving train. Even once they managed to climb aboard, Blackeye had hoped his comrades would be able to deal with the intruders without losing more time getting to town. Yet, once he heard Roberta's enraged screams followed by gunfire and silence, he knew something had gone terribly wrong and ordered the engineer to stop the train dead in its tracks. It might have seemed irrational to some but Blackeye knew that if the lawmen were still alive when the train reached Dry Heat, it was possible that backup would be waiting. That was a risk Blackeye was not willing to take. This was a fight that would be fought on the tracks, in the vicinity of no town.

As soon as the engineer stopped the train, Blackeye hit him on the back of the head with the handle of his pistol. He needed the engineer alive to drive the train into town later, but he didn't have time to tie him up. He couldn't take the risk of having him escape but, if he was merely unconscious, he would be both useful and out of the way. Blackeye reckoned that the engineer would come to in about a half hour with nothing more serious than a bruise and a sore head. Leaving the engineer lying unconscious at the foot of the controls, Blackeye gripped a pistol in each hand and burst into the next room.

Andy and Phil were ready for him. As soon as Blackeye started shooting they returned fire. Yet Blackeye was skilled at gunfights and he used the doorway to the engine room for a shield as Phil and Andy dove behind sacks of mail. No man was willing to back down as they entered into what was to become the most memorable gunfight of their lives.

Three cars back on the train trouble reigned. The black cowboys and the two deputies had discovered the passenger car where most of the hostages were being held. The second they walked into the room Leroy, Amanda, Danny, and Arnold—who had just returned from raiding the train—started shooting. Through their gags the hostages screamed, terrified as bullets flew in every direction.

Ron had never seen such chaos. Gunsmoke filled the air as Hubbards jumped over hostages as if they were steppingstones in a mad man's dream. They were 'yee-hawing' and celebrating the prospect of a good gunfight. Despite the choking smoke, the flying bullets, and the stress of aiming just right, Ron couldn't help but be chilled to the bone by the smiling—almost joyous— Hubbards. It seemed that fighting made them happier than spoiled children on Christmas day. *They're insane,* he realized, *totally insane.*

Beside Ron, Jack yelped with pain. Ron looked over to see that Jack had been hit with a bullet in the right side of his stomach. Clayton was calling to him and asking if he was okay. Despite his obvious agony, Jack was nodding and shooting as if he wasn't hurting one bit. Danny had been shot in the leg and Leroy's shoulder was wounded, but they seemed unfazed by their injuries. Both the Hubbard men were laughing and screaming as they fired their weapons. Watching them, Ron wondered if all this could have been prevented if the desert had an insane asylum.

Amanda wasn't like her cousins. She was smart and serious when it came to battle, and her aim was deadly. The only look on her face was that of determination and she had cleverly turned a table onto its side so she could protect herself from bullets. A bad situation got worse when James, Wallace, and Max walked into the room equipped with mail sacks filled with stolen goods. When they entered the passenger car and saw the shootout, they used their filled sacks as full body shields and started firing at the lawmen.

Amanda was quick to catch onto a good idea. Seeing how easily her cousins could move with portable shields, Amanda grabbed a bound hostage—a terrified, middle-aged woman in a flower-print pink dress. Using the woman as a shield, Amanda emerged from behind the table and crept toward the door to the car behind the passenger area.

"Hold your fire at the woman!" Ron screamed. "She's got a hostage! Cover me, I'm goin' after her!"

"I'll go too!" Jonas replied, following the deputy. With Carl, Pete, Sam, Jack, and Clayton distracting the other Hubbards, Ron and Jonas were able to follow Amanda and her hostage into the next room. Ron could hear the hostage sobbing as Amanda dragged her through the

train and shot over her shoulder. Even in the midst
of panic, Amanda's aim was unfortunately good—one of
her bullets struck Ron in the leg causing him to fall with
a cry of pain.

"Hold on, Deputy!" Jonas bellowed, helping Ron up.

"I'm okay, follow her, I'll be able to drag myself
along an' meet you. Go, we can't lose sight of her. An'
be careful!"

Reluctantly, Jonas left the wounded deputy's side
and followed the two women through the train, desperately dodging bullets and muttering prayers as he went.
Although Jonas carried a gun he rarely fired it, and it
was inconceivable to him to actually shoot another human being. Not wanting to end a life, Jonas called to
Amanda, trying to reason with her.

"You don't got to do this," he cried, "put the woman
down! She didn't do nothin' to you!"

Jonas' pleas were answered with flying bullets.
Amanda wasn't discussing anything. Her face was distorted into an enraged snarl and her trigger finger was
doing the talking. She fired bullets insanely, trying to
hit Jonas until her gun jammed. Cussing and shaking
the gun in fury, Amanda fixed Jonas with a toothy snarl
before dragging the hostage by the hair farther back
into the train.

"Now that you done run out of bullets let the lady go!"
Jonas proclaimed, trying to keep the tremble out of his
voice as he held his gun up toward Amanda. She responded by throwing her gun at him. The metal connected with the side of Jonas' eye causing him to stumble

backwards in pain. As Jonas struggled for balance, Amanda finally came upon the door she had been looking for—the engineers' sleeping area—and frantically began to bang on it.

"Katie!" Amanda screamed, "Katie, we got trouble!"

"We got trouble 'cause yo' causin' trouble!" Jonas shouted. "Hurtin' somebody ain't gonna prove nothin'. We all the Lord's children, now let that woman be!"

"You want me to free her?" Amanda snarled savagely turning to face Jonas. "Fine, I'll free her from my grip an' this train an' even this life!"

Smiling wickedly, Amanda pulled out a knife and held it to the hostage's throat. Jonas watched horrorstruck, trying to make himself pull the trigger of his gun but unable to bring himself to shoot. Seconds before Amanda could murder the hostage, a shot rang out. With a look of surprise, rage, and shock on her face, Amanda Hubbard fell to the floor, dead. Before the hostage could fall with her, Jonas grabbed the woman away from Amanda's body.

Ron stood behind Jonas, holding his smoking gun. He had hobbled to the scene on his wounded leg. Unlike the freed slave, the deputy had no qualms about shooting Amanda to save the hostage. Seconds after Amanda's lifeless body fell, Katie opened the door—holding Cynthia in front of her like a prize—and looked upon the body of her sister at her feet.

"Amanda!" Katie wailed, kneeling toward her sister and cruelly pulling Cynthia down beside her by her hair. Jonas knew that Katie would only be distracted for a few seconds and he took advantage of the time by taking a step toward the girl. Sensing movement, Katie struck like a viper. She quickly leaped up and aimed her weapon, ready to shoot Jonas. Then she heard Ron cock his gun.

"If you shoot him I'll shoot you, an' I don't wanna do that," the deputy declared firmly.

Katie flashed him a cold, cruel grin and, as quick as a wink, turned the gun on Cynthia. "Y'all took my husband first an' now you've killed my favorite sister!" she screeched, still smiling wolfishly yet unable to hold back enraged tears. "Where's the sheriff? If y'all don't bring me to him right now, I swear I'll kill this girl right here. Even if you shoot me, pullin' this trigger will be my last act."

"We know where the sheriff is!" Ron declared hastily. "We'll take you to him right now if you promise not to hurt Cynthia."

"Maybe," Katie spat, painfully tightening her grip on Cynthia. "Put down your weapon, Deputy, an' maybe I won't hurt this little girl none on our way to see her uncle."

Ron quickly obeyed. Favoring his wounded leg, Jonas helped him walk to the front of the train, thus leading the way for Katie and Cynthia.

As soon as Amanda grabbed the hostage and ran from the passenger area chaos erupted in the room. Jack, despite being woozy from blood loss and growing weaker by the second, relentlessly shot at Danny. Sam and Leroy were involved in a face-off as Clayton fought Arnold. Carl and Pete fought side by side against James, Wallace, and Max who, blessedly, had terrible aim. It was a violent, hectic fight; worse than anything Jack had ever seen—even on the battlefields of the Civil War. The air was so thick with gunsmoke that it was hard to see. Sam barely saw Leroy run past him, leaping over hostages and heading toward the engine room. Sam followed him, happy to be out of the eye-tearing, smoke-filled passenger area. Both Sam and Leroy fired and dodged bullets as they chased each other through the mail train.

As they approached the room where Andy, Phil, and Blackeye were battling it out, Leroy stumbled and fell. Sam took immediate advantage and tried to wrestle the gun out of the Hubbard's hand. Neither Leroy nor Sam were willing to give up their weapons and, before Sam was fully aware of what was happening, they were rolling on the floor underneath the hail of the older men's gunfire.

They stopped once they reached the inside of the engine room. Finally, in an area free of gunfire, Sam and Leroy leaped to their feet, drew their weapons, and fired at the same point-blank range. In what could only be described as a bizarre coincidence, both guns 'clicked,' signifying their lack of ammunition. For a moment the two men looked at each other dumbfounded; then Leroy was coming at Sam with a knife in his hand. It happened so quickly that Sam was caught off guard and unprepared for the attack. Terror swept through him as he prepared himself for the fatal pierce of the knife.

Then Sam saw Leroy pitch forward to the floor—landing on the wrong end of his knife. Sam was surprised to see that his savior was the engineer who had regained consciousness just in time to knock Leroy square over the head with a coffee cup.

Phil never saw Leroy and Sam come rolling through the room; he didn't have time to notice anything while involved in a gunfight with Blackeye. The bandit was an excellent marksman and, despite his considerable age, he was quick and agile. He was good at maneuvering around a room and he knew how to turn any object in the area into a shield. Although Andy, Phil, and Blackeye had all been shooting at each other for a good ten minutes, no one had yet been hit although Phil's wounded arm had re-opened. Phil could not remember the last time he had been so tense. He was sure that he would meet his maker before this fight was over—it seemed as if both he and Andy together were not enough to handle Blackeye. They had been dancing around the room, shooting and fighting and cussing for what seemed like an eternity. Andy was stuck in the corner reloading his weapon when he noticed that there was a small mirror mounted in the top right corner of the room. Phil was standing to the far left of the mirror crouching behind a mail sack and shooting at Blackeye, who was facing him and shooting with one hand while holding a thick wooden chair up to catch bullets for him in the other.

Maybe, just maybe, if Phil shoots that mirror the

glass will rain down on Blackeye's face an' distract him just long enough so I can shoot him, Andy thought.

Blackeye's back was turned to the sheriff of Cattle Skull and so he did not notice Andy catch Phil's eye and mouth the word *mirror* while pointing up to the corner where the mirror was mounted. Although Andy was the more observant of the two men, Phil's lip-reading skills never failed him and he immediately knew what Andy was suggesting when he saw the mirror. Without hesitation, Phil aimed for the mirror and sent shards of glass raining on Blackeye's face. Blackeye screamed and dropped his weapon in order to defend his remaining eye from the glass. At that very moment, both Phil and Andy fired their weapons and hit Blackeye dead on. The big, one-eyed man fell with a resounding crash, never to rise again. Instantly, Phil and Andy emerged from behind their cover to inspect the body and there was no doubt about it—Bernie 'Blackeye' Crawdrum was finally dead.

"I knew you could make that shot," Andy remarked to Phil. "Your eyes ain't changed much since we was kids. I remember you shootin' holes in glasses an' readin' whole sentences from lips to impress girls."

"Whoever woulda thought them party tricks woulda come in handy for gettin' rid of this guy? Now for the big question: Where's my niece?"

By the time Katie marched toward the engine room with Cynthia she was the last living Hubbard aboard the train. Although her family had outnumbered the lawmen and their posse by eleven to nine, the majority of the Hubbards had poor shooting skills, which had been made worse by their consumption of stolen liquor. Their intoxication had cost them their lives. As Katie walked through the train and saw the remains of her kin, she decided that she would kill herself after putting a bullet in the girl and the sheriff. What was the point of living if she was captured and hanged? Death by her own hand would be better, much better. Perhaps in death she would finally be with her beloved Dwayne.

The hate that rose inside of Katie when she laid eyes on Sheriff Phil was white-hot. It was as if her anger was a live animal trapped inside of her, viciously attempting to claw it's way out and shatter her one remaining pillar of sanity. When Katie entered the room, Phil did not even notice her look of loathing, he was simply staring at his niece, stunned. Cynthia *did* look like him, *a lot* like him, and it made Phil weak with terror when he realized that Katie was holding a gun to the girl's head. Seeing that Phil was having difficulty finding his voice, Andy took a few tentative steps toward Katie.

"You're surrounded," he declared. "You best let that girl go so we can talk this out rationally."

Katie replied by pushing the nozzle of the gun more firmly into the side of Cynthia's head and threateningly wrapping her finger around the trigger.

"I ain't discussin' nothin' with nobody but Sheriff Palmer here," she hissed. "We have us some talkin' to do an' it don't concern you." Katie faced Phil and gestured toward the engine room. "Get in there."

Phil did not argue. He obediently turned and walked into the engine room, wary about turning his back on Katie but even more wary about enraging her further. Sam and the engineer wasted no time exiting when they realized what was happening. Once Phil, Katie, and Cynthia were alone, Katie slammed the door shut, seemingly indifferent to the presence of Leroy's body. Phil wasted no time in pleading for Cynthia. Normally, he would never be reduced to pleading, but when it came to Cynthia he wasn't too proud to beg.

"Katie, whatever this is about, whatever your reasons, Cynthia has nothin' to do with it. Please let her go, she didn't do nothin' to you."

"I could say the same thing to you about my husband," Katie replied coldly.

"Katie—"

"It don't feel good, do it?" Katie crackled, immensely enjoying the sheriff's torment. "You ain't too keen on havin' somebody you care about payin' for your mistakes, huh? Well, this is how it feels, Sheriff."

"What are you talkin' about?"

"You know exactly what I'm talkin' about! The tables have turned an' I'm in charge now! You thought you could get revenge on me for stayin' around your town by killin' Dwayne! You got your revenge, but you ain't gonna get away with it!"

"Katie, I swear on the Bible that Dwayne's death was an accident."

"You're still stickin' to that story? You think I'm mighty stupid, don't you? You think I'm just gonna believe anythin' an' free this girl just so you can laugh at me before shootin' me dead! An' that's what you wanted to do to begin with, ain't it? To see me dead! Y'all killed my whole family, includin' my favorite sister today! But it's my husband you're gonna pay for!"

"Katie, I swear I didn't do nothin' to hurt Dwayne."

"Yes, you did!" Katie half screamed, half sobbed, tears streaming down her face. "It was all you—you planned all of it! Who asked for posse volunteers knowin' Dwayne would come runnin' to help? You! Who led my husband up that mountain? You! Who was the one who sicced that rattler on him? You! You, you, you—it was all you plottin' to ruin my life!"

As she screamed this accusation, Katie Hubbard Roberts lost all semblance of composure. She moved the nozzle of the gun away from Cynthia and pointed it at Phil. Dropping the girl to the floor, she hesitated for a second to blink the tears out of her eyes before shooting Phil at point-blank range. That single moment was all Phil needed to draw and fire. He shot Katie through the heart milliseconds after her bullet flew into his chest. Katie and Phil fell to the ground at the same time. The last fleeting memory to run through Katie's mind before her life ended was Dwayne's sweet smile.

All Phil felt was pain—searing agony in his chest right over his heart. He was sure that he was seconds away from death, yet he felt no sense of peace or fading away—all he felt was throbbing soreness. Slowly, he became aware that he was lying on the floor and the small engine room was full of people. Tentatively, Phil opened his eyes to see Ron's concerned face leaning over him. Summoning up great strength, every move instigating massive pain, Phil raised his hand and felt his chest. He expected to feel his blood spreading over him but he neither felt nor saw any blood.

"Chest," he muttered to Ron.

"She shot right at your heart," Ron replied. "She aimed perfectly too. You'd be dead right now if it wasn't for these." Ron pulled the sheriff's thick pack of cards out of the front pocket of his shirt. A single bullet had been shot squarely into the middle of the pack. It stopped more than halfway through.

So I ain't dead, just lookin' at a nasty bruise, Phil thought as Ron helped him up. "Where's Cynthia?" Phil asked frantically.

"She's fine," Ron replied holding his wounded leg, "she's right over there. She's frightened but she ain't injured. You got Katie, Phil, we got 'em all. They're gone. You gave us all a good scare though. When we heard the gunshots we came runnin' in, thinkin' that somethin' had gone bad an' you was a goner. Thank the Lord we was wrong."

Phil hardly heard the deputy's words. He was staring at Cynthia, who was sitting on the floor, still tied and gagged, sobbing and flinching away from anyone who approached her. She was darting her eyes around surveying the scene in a rapid, terrified manner. *Oh you poor little thing,* Phil thought as he walked toward his niece. *You poor, poor, little girl.*

Grief and regret engulfed the sheriff. He had known

that taking Cynthia to Dry Heat was a mistake but he had agreed to bring her to New Mexico anyway. He had wanted nothing more than to make everything perfect for her and he had instead, unwillingly, led her into a hijacking and hostage situation. *She'll never be right again after this, not after losin' her parents an' brother an' all too. Oh God, I'm sorry Clyde, I'm so sorry.*

As Phil approached his niece she shrank further back, as if she was trying to disappear into the wall. Her hazel eyes were alive with fear, and the closer Phil got to her, the more frightened she became. *What did Katie say to her about me? She looks more frightened than a calf caught in a fence.*

"It's okay, Cynthia," Phil declared, trying his hardest to sound reassuring. "It's all over now. I promise nothing is ever gonna hurt you again. From now on everything's all right, your Uncle Phil promises you that."

Cynthia was still staring at him fearfully and whimpering. When Phil leaned down to undo her restraints she uttered a small cry, as if she expected him to strike her. "It's okay now, Cynthia, I promise it's all okay now."

Even once the girl was untied, she did not speak; she only stared at Phil and the other men fearfully. Phil could think of nothing else to do aside from speaking to her in the most comforting tone of voice he could muster. He feared that she wasn't listening to him—or wasn't capable of understanding him—that, somehow due to the trauma, her mind had shut down. Blessedly, after a few minutes, her eyes welled with tears and she started to sob harder than ever, falling into her uncle's arms.

And so, at long last, Phil was acquainted with his niece. He held her in his arms and wished that he could reverse the day, unable to hold back a tear or two for his niece's suffering. Phil didn't comment or stir when the engineer started up the train and headed to Dry Heat for assistance. All that mattered to the sheriff was comforting his terrified but alive niece, his last living relative, his family.

Chapter Sixteen

It had been over a month since Cynthia's turbulent arrival in Dry Heat. As he sat on his office porch, relaxing in the glow of the setting afternoon sun, Phil looked back on that day with wonder. It had been the most frightening and hectic day of his life and he couldn't believe that he, and everyone he cared about, had survived it.

When the train pulled into the Dry Heat station half the town was waiting to assist the wounded. Dr. Noonan was on hand to immediately administer care to Jack, who was barely conscious and near death. The hostages had been released relatively unharmed, still Dr. Noonan had demanded that some of them be taken in for examination due mainly to hysteria and gunsmoke inhalation. A few hostages suffered from temporary hearing loss due to all the shooting and a number had sore limbs from having been stepped on during the passenger car shootout. The bodies of the Hubbards had been removed from the train and buried outside of town. For years to come the story of the crazy Hubbard clan would be a favorite topic of campfire fables intended to frighten youngsters.

The posse's horses had run back toward Dry Heat after being abandoned near the train. They were captured by a group of local ranchers who kept them safe until ownership was claimed. Phil could not describe how happy he was when he heard that all the horses had been found unharmed and returned so quickly. It was a blessing to look into the corral and see Crow safe and sound and happily eating oats.

Understandably, Cynthia had been a nervous wreck when she first came to town. She was so quiet the first few days that Phil feared she had been frightened into muteness. At first Cynthia was wary of Phil and made it a point to give him a wide berth while shooting distrustful glances in his direction. Yet, after a week, she had warmed up to her uncle enough to play a game of cards with him. She slept with the doll he bought her and she seemed to like her room. On a few occasions Phil had even managed to make her crack a smile.

Phil supposed that Maggie was part of the reason why Cynthia had started trusting him. When Maggie heard that the mail train had been hijacked she had come into town to check on Phil and had seen how anxious Cynthia appeared. Maggie could tell that Phil was at a loss for what to do and she had made it her mission to venture into town each day and spend a few hours visiting Phil and Cynthia. She cooked and sewed with her and talked to her about horses and the desert life and anything else that entered into her head. Although Cynthia had been silent company for the first few days, she soon warmed to Maggie enough to start and carry the conversation. Cynthia liked having Maggie around and so did Phil. Although he was hesitant to say they were courting, he had made it a point to take Maggie out walking on more than one occasion, and they saw each other on a daily basis. Phil had no way of knowing where their relationship would lead but he could easily see Maggie becoming a big part of his life.

Since the departure of Larry and his men the town had become a much nicer place. For starters, no one dared to call Maggie mad and she and her Navajo friends were welcomed. Jack, Clayton, Jonas, Sam, and Pete had also found acceptance throughout Dry Heat. Willis Lauder had become an instant friend to the five men once he learned that they were the ones responsible for Lloyd's rescue and safe return. The ex–slaves spent their days doing odd jobs alongside other town ranch hands and enjoying free life on the range.

Within the month, Dry Heat had seen more changes than it ever had before. Mayor Don Rombert had finally "retired" to Claire's Cactus, and Phil was now Mayor Phil. Ron had been elevated to Sheriff Harris and, as his first act as sheriff, had awarded Hawk the title of Deputy Murray. Although Ron's leg was still healing and he walked with a limp, he had managed to take Carrie, his fiancée, out dancing on three occasions.

Ron had proposed to Carrie the same day as the hijacking. He had popped the question while he was in the doctor's quarters having his leg bandaged. Although Carrie had quickly accepted Ron's offer, she had been wary about remaining in Dry Heat. Carrie had been deeply, emotionally scarred by how quickly the majority of the townspeople had turned on her under Larry and Clarence. For a few weeks after the incident Carrie had been withdrawn and easily startled. Even after the engagement, Carrie had shown a desire to leave Dry Heat, yet everyone in town seemed to be searching for a new start and a second chance. Claire offered Carrie her dream job: Create and star in her own one-woman show which would be performed three nights a week on the saloon stage. The offer had been too good to pass up, and Carrie agreed to remain in town. Phil reckoned that it would be a long time before Carrie felt completely at ease—no one gets over an execution threat quickly—yet he supposed that her marriage to Ron, and her show, would certainly hasten the readjustment process.

Although Phil assumed Carrie would readjust hastily, he wondered if the same could be said for the man who would be marrying her and Ron in a few weeks' time. Since the death of his nephew, Preacher Warren Harden had become a shell of his old self. He was a lost, broken man who had difficulty finding a way to redeem himself for his nephew's actions. No one in Dry Heat blamed Warren for what happened and they encouraged him to stay by attending service in full and bringing him small gifts such as eggs and cookies to show they cared about him. The Gardeners were especially good at making sure that the preacher wanted for nothing by supplying him with items from their general store. Ever since Hugh made a speedy recovery from his arrow wound, the Gardeners had become faithful churchgoers. Phil hoped that Warren would be able to move on. The preacher was a good man who had been dealt a bad hand with that nephew of his. He deserved happiness after all those long, hard years.

Since Larry left, everyone had been putting extra emphasis on community harmony. Phil was touched by the large number of people who had gone out of their way to make Cynthia feel welcome. Peggy Cobwey knitted her colorful cotton dresses, and Carrie offered to teach her how to dance. Cynthia was well educated and, since she knew how to read and write at a level far above the other children in town, Wendy Philips had given her a job as an assistant schoolteacher. To show appreciation toward her rescuers, Cynthia taught the black cowboys how to read and write—knowledge which had never before been offered to them. Phil liked the idea of Cynthia being a schoolteacher, especially since Dry Heat's population was growing. A few weeks after Cynthia's arrival, Nick Stooker's wife, Rose, gave birth to twins; a boy and a girl named Sean and Abigail.

Phil leaned back against the porch steps and smiled as the fading sunlight caressed his face. Andy and Carl were due to arrive any minute for a night of poker and harmonica playing. Ever since they were youngsters

Phil had teased Andy about his lackluster harmonica skills but, deep down, Phil enjoyed the melodies. Plus, he had always been the better poker player, and he usually managed to win a few bucks from his best friend.

This is the way life oughta be, no worries about anythin' but off-key harmonica playin' an' gainin' braggin' rights by winnin' in poker.

Phil smiled. Proud to be the mayor of the small, harmonious, town known as Dry Heat.